THE QUESTION OF MAX
AMANDA CROSS
A Kate Fansler Mystery

Also by Amanda Cross
Published by Ballantine Books:

DEATH IN A TENURED POSITION

THE JAMES JOYCE MURDER

THE QUESTION OF MAX

Amanda Cross

BALLANTINE BOOKS • NEW YORK

Grateful acknowledgment is made to Harcourt Brace Jovano-
vich, Inc., New York, and to Faber and Faber Ltd., London,
for permission to quote from T. S. Eliot's poem "Little Gidding"
from *Four Quartets;* and to the Marvell Press, London, for permission to quote from Philip Larkin's poem "Wants" from his
collection *The Less Deceived.*

Library of Congress Catalog Card Number: 76-2561

ISBN 0-345-32897-3

This edition published by arrangement with
Alfred A. Knopf, Inc.

Printed in Canada

First Ballantine Books Edition: May 1984
Second Printing: June 1985

To Joan Ferrante

Art, if it doesn't start there, at least ends,
Whether aesthetics like the thought or not,
In an attempt to entertain our friends.
W. H. Auden

THE QUESTION
OF MAX

part one

March

one

Kate Fansler's life had achieved, within the last year, a neat division between urban elegance and rural simplicity, even if, as was certain, the rural simplicity was a lot simpler than the urban elegance was elegant. Her farmer neighbors observed with ill-concealed scorn her one-room cabin and unmowed grass, while her urban associates placed her on the scale of elegance only so far as their own eyes could reach. If she appeared easily affluent to her colleagues, she was considered, by those of her mother's generation who chanced to come across her, to be close to slumming. At this particular moment in March, she was priding herself on the sharp contradictions in her life, those contradictions which gave flavor to experience and rest to the soul. Such sharp contradictions, of course, require a dexterity bordering upon gymnastics. With a sense, therefore, of an acrobat whose muscles have suddenly frozen, Kate watched Maximillian Reston search in vain the uncut meadow surrounding her cabin for a path to her door.

Max was the last person in the world to whom a wild rural retreat would hold any attraction. But even had her country refuge been run on the elegant lines of Edith Wharton's famous turn-of-the-century mansion

11

not far distant in the Berkshires, Reston's unannounced approach would have been a cause for astonishment. He was not a man given to excursions into other people's lives. Their work, yes. Friendship, or what passed with Max for friendship, allowed response in beautifully contrived letters to the publications of one's friends. But intimacy he considered a contemporary fall from grace as regrettable as the loss of manners, formality, and sartorial distinctions between the sexes.

Kate, looking down at her mud-stained sneakers and ancient blue-jeans, considered several mad escapes. She could run straight out the back door into the woods and there lurk undiscovered until Max departed. But when and, more importantly, how would he depart? He had dismissed the taxi which had deposited him upon her road, and her house contained no telephone with which to summon another. Flight seemed inadvisable. Disguise? Suppose she were to pretend to be a tramp or a besotted old woman mumbling about goblins . . . Not bad, that, but it presented the same problem as the first alternative. How would Max depart? Nothing for it, perhaps, but to face the man. And Max, once he had seen her in this state, in this house, she who had never dined with him or talked with him in any elegance less than that provided by his club (on those few evenings when his club admitted the other sex to its sacred precincts), would he leave her cabin and her life forever? With a pang, Kate realized that she would regret the loss of him. Damn and blast Max.

Unaware of the curse directed toward him, Reston looked for a moment down the rutted road, longing, perhaps, for his now departed taxi. One could observe, even at this distance, the moment when he had decided to plunge across the meadow to the greater civilization, he supposed, that lay within the cabin. Kate thought wildly of changing her clothes. But the dishonesty of this disgusted her, nor was she positively beguiled at the thought of being found by Max in, so to speak, the chrysalis stage of nudity. I must stand my ground, she muttered to herself, tucking back the loose strands of hair.

The question was, how had Max found her? She had known him an expert in all the byways of civilization, but rural ingenuity she would not have expected. Cautiously, but accepting her fate, Kate went to the door and opened it, watching Max pick his way across the muddy meadow. When he was still ten feet away, she spoke: "There are two questions. How you found me, and why? It is perhaps unfeeling of me, but I think I am more intrigued by the first."

"Guy told me about it," Max said, stepping inside and viewing the cabin with a critical scrutiny he made no attempt to disguise. "He also told me that Reed had given it to you. When you failed to turn up in any civilized place, I decided to try this on a long shot."

"Did Guy describe exactly in which Berkshire wood it lay?"

"Of course not. He mentioned the nearest town, from where I made inquiries about an isolated cabin and a lunatic woman. Do you have drinking water that runs from a faucet, or must one throw oneself down beside a babbling brook?"

"There are faucets," Kate said. "Sit down and I will get you a drink of water. I'm afraid there is nothing else I can offer you, except tea from a bag, coffee of the instant variety, or California wine."

13

With visible effort, Max restrained a shudder. "Water will be excellent," he said. He stared about him and Kate looked at the cabin through his eyes. It consisted of one large room with a vaulted ceiling, beneath which, on one side, was a sleeping balcony. For furniture there was another mattress on legs, covered with pillows and a throw, for sitting. Two overstuffed chairs of the sort someone had obviously decided to do away with when he came into money, and a round deal table with two straight chairs completed the furnishings.

"Guy said he and Reed built this with their own hands," Max said, dropping with a mixture of relief and distaste into one of the deep chairs, whose innards hit the floor as they felt his weight. Max was not the sort of man to loll, and he contrived to look more uncomfortable than he would have in a straight-backed chair of rigid proportions. Still, he had found Kate, which said a good deal for his perseverance and, one supposed, for the seriousness of his intentions. What these could possibly be Kate forbore even to imagine.

Max seemed strangely reluctant to come to the point of his extraordinary visit. "This looks as though someone built it with his bare hands."

"Guy built it, with only occasional help from Reed. I thought he told you?"

"One gathered it was of his own devising. He didn't go into details, and I somehow assumed supervision rather than actual fabrication."

"Guy has been Reed's friend for a long time," Kate said. "Years before Reed and I were married, Guy had a breakdown. What is described by the doctors as a 'moderate depression.' Caused, if depressions can ever be said to have a cause, by what the poets call 'the melancholy of all things completed.' As an advertising man, Guy had great success very young. There was the usual psychotherapy, the usual drugs, but he cured himself or, more accurately, guided himself out of the trouble through work. Manual work. Here. Guy had inherited these woods, oh, years ago. He started to build this house more or less in the middle of his acres, with Reed's help. He said that Reed's quiet presence and assistance had saved him. Later, when he was well again, he sold Reed the house and land, and Reed gave it to me for a retreat. 'It saved Guy,' he said, 'and it may you.' Not that I was collapsing, just nervy. Naturally Guy told you none of this."

"Naturally," Max said, his tone speaking volumes.

"Well, if you want discretion, Max, and the decency of keeping one's feelings to oneself, you've come to the wrong place. I didn't say person, I said place. I'm here alone much of the time, but alone or not, I play no games. This place saves one."

"From what?" Max asked, getting up to look out. "From civilization, I suppose. From gracious living, courtesy, style, and decent demeanor."

"Oh, Max, what a snob you are. I know all the metaphors about ill-tended gardens, with the hedges a thicket, the weeds in the drive, and the wind whistling in the trees. I prefer my nature wild, and don't find it gloomy or demoralizing. In fact, I suspect this is what the Garden of Eden was like, if you want to know. No doubt most people think it resembled an expensive golf course. Can you imagine how many birds I have here in summer, because of the thickets? Of course it's not your style but, if I may assume what I'm sure you would not call decent demeanor, I never supposed it was nor would have dreamed of submitting you to this wilderness, nor to me within it."

"My dear, of course." Max struggled to reassume his wonted courtesy. "Perhaps I had better telephone for my taxi to return. I ought not to have tracked you down in this obtrusive way, and then criticized . . ."

"There *is* no telephone. I thought you'd grasped the fact that I'm away from it all."

"But what if there was an emergency?"

"Most emergencies are so only in the eyes of those having them, and can await my attentions. Suppose, after all, I were climbing in the Yukon. Reed and one or two of my most intimate friends know of a number down the road. It is that of a grasping and narrow-minded woman who has been promised a large reward for every time she comes and tells me of a call. There have not been many. When you decide to leave I shall drive you to town, and throw myself upon your mercies not to tell anyone where you found me, or how. Do you want to go now?"

"Might I have a cup of tea after all?"

Kate rose to her feet to comply with this request. "Perhaps," she said to Max, "you would be more comfortable at the table. I do have a proper bathroom, by the way, in case you were wondering."

"Did Guy put that in, too?"

"No. Guy built all this, but without indoor plumbing or an actual road in through the woods. I added these, and the Franklin stove over there."

"Do you mean you come up here in the winter?"

"Of course. Its beauty cannot be imagined, though the silence, which used to be its greatest attraction, has been shattered. Don't get me started on that. Those

16

lunatic snowmobiles, screaming through the night with the noise of a buzz saw, disturbing hibernating animals and ruining people's lawns. Fences are no protection from them, but woods, fortunately, are. And then there is a damn snow-making machine on some blasted ski slope, miles from here, but on a clear night I'm sure they can hear it in Schenectady. My lawyer is making inquiries." Kate brought in the teacups and placed them on the table. "There is sugar, if you take it. People suppose I come away to commune with some spirit, my own or another. And I do, in a way. But I spend an unconscionable amount of time dreaming of the eradication of the internal combustion engine. A system of planes and railroads, great public transportation in the cities, bicycles for those who choose to pedal, and horses and buggies for the aged, the infirm, and the nostalgic. How does it strike you?"

"I don't think it will ever catch on."

"Alas, no. But who is to stop me dreaming of General Motors converting to electrically powered urban transportation? Max, what on earth brought you here? Even if you didn't know I was roughing it quite to this extent, you might have known you wouldn't find me in something like the Oak Room at the Plaza."

"I hoped," Max said, stirring his tea and gazing into the distance, "to persuade you to take a trip with me. Now," he added. "In your car," he finally concluded, as though to get all the outrage on the table between them at once.

Kate stared at the man. Had the president of the university or, for that matter, the shah of Iran turned up with such a suggestion, she would not have more readily begun, with an anxious pang, to doubt her own

17

sanity. Or could Max, elegant, controlled, brilliant Max, have gone all suddenly and unexpectedly round the bend? Max must have seen a look of apprehension pass over her face.

"An odd request, I know," he said, pushing back his chair and crossing his long, elegantly trousered legs. Max was one of these men who would as soon have walked the streets in his underwear as reveal any flesh between his socks and trousers. Kate—and this was one of the more acrobatic features of her inconsistent nature—admired this. She tried, nobly, not to draw any conclusions about character from the kind of socks a man wore—that would be ridiculous—but at the same time she could not help noticing socks. Reed, who agreed with her in the matter of socks, comforted her in this strange intolerance. "I," he informed her in consoling tones, "cannot abide red nail polish. One must tolerate oneself." There is no question, Kate thought, I am beginning to think in the sort of stream of consciousness written by second-rate writers under the influence of imitators of Virginia Woolf.

"An odd request indeed," Kate said, concentrating her thoughts. "Where did you have in mind to flee to?"

"Not flee," Max said. "Visit. The coast of Maine. Cecily's house."

"Now? Didn't she die a short time ago? In England?" Never mind the length of his socks, Kate mused. Of what length are his thoughts?

Max, having asked and received permission to smoke, lit a cigarette in a style that had departed, one thought, with the late Noel Coward. Suddenly Kate felt better. After all, Max, whatever his prejudices—and they were, God knew, both vehement and reactionary—was the sanest man she knew, no doubt because he was so absolutely certain about everything. Kate had once remarked of Max that she wished she were as certain of anything as Max was of everything, a comment originally made of Macaulay. Conversation with Max, despite this, was lively and interesting; one steered through his prejudices as through a mined harbor, but the view and the breeze were rewarding. A professor of art history, Max was equally renowned for his achievements as a scholar and his elegance as a bachelor and man about town. Widely disliked and envied, he had the talent of befriending anyone who appealed to him. These were not many, but they were always an interesting lot. Kate, received from the frigid hinterlands into the still chilly regions of acquaintanceship, had developed over the years a profound affection for Max. She dined with him, talked with him, exchanged with him witty letters which cost her, she suspected, more effort than they cost him. But the only trip she had ever expected to take with Max was in a taxi, being dropped home by him on his way to his elegant flat in Turtle Bay.

"I'll tell you all about it in a minute," Max said. "Tell me about all this. . . ." He waved his cigarette. "I didn't know you went in for depressions. But then, before the advent of Reed, I didn't know you went in for marriage."

"Spoken like a true bachelor," Kate said, "with just the proper tone of regret. Yet you know perfectly well if I weren't married, you would never have arrived here and asked me to drive off with you into darkest Maine."

"The coast," Max said. "Not darkest. It is true one

is more comfortable with married women, but there are always exceptions. You are one."

"You are not. I have noticed that bachelors are far more fun to dine with than married men, even if one could dine with a married man unaccompanied by wife, which usually one can't. Why do you think marriage has such a dreadful effect upon men's conversation, their manners, and their wit?"

"Because bachelors must earn their supper by being charming."

"Balderdash. You could resign from the university tomorrow and never have to earn another supper by any means whatever."

"Perhaps. Reed's conversation, manners, and wit seemed satisfactory to me."

"And to me, praise the Lord. I come here from time to time not to escape Reed, but myself. Reed is a miracle in understanding that, and in giving me this place. Yet Reed is not frightened by intimacy and you are. Perhaps the wit of bachelors is a defense against humanity. How little we ever know about people."

"A fact I have always roundly applauded. Surely one can have conversation with someone of similar tastes and intelligence without examining, in turn, the most agonizing details of each other's intimate psyche."

"Well, I don't agree about conversation, but I do about life in general. Which is why I am here, seeking an absence from the domination of things and the expectation of people."

"I completely deserve that and humbly apologize."

"Are we to drive from here to Maine without examining our psyches at least to the extent of learning why? Particularly since we are to travel in my car? You did mention that."

"Well, either in your car or in one we might rent in town. I didn't, you know, tell Reed I was coming. He didn't give away your location, but accepted with a certain amount of grace the knowledge that I would seek you out. I explained to him about Cecily."

"My heart beats as one with Reed's, but we are not in telepathic communication. You were not to gather that from the absence of a telephone."

"Asperity suits you, Kate. Better than that dreadful male and oversized shirt. The great, cool, imperturbable Max Reston does not want to visit Cecily's house alone. I throw myself upon your mercy. The neighbors up there think there may have been intruders. As her literary executor, I must go. As a man, I'm funking it alone. My need of you, while it partakes more of admiration than of passion, is intense. Would you come with me now? We can spend the night at a quiet civilized inn in a charming town on the coast, if you will honor me?"

"Suppose these jeans and this large, male, ill-fitting shirt were all I had to wear?"

"You shall not escape that easily," Max said. "Besides, you forget that I know your breeding. You will have, at the very least, an elegant pantsuit in that closet. Kate dear, you are about to earn my eternal gratitude. I shall send you a magnificent present from Cartier's, and wait all my life for the chance to do you an equally gallant service."

"You'd better begin," Kate said, "if I am to spare your blushes, by smoking outside. I do not intend to don my elegant pantsuit in the bathroom. Can you drive?"

"Alas, no," Max said, bowing his way out, as though he were leaving an Edwardian drawing room in Belgravia. "But as you drive, I shall divert you on the way with tales about Cecily."

"Cecily Hutchins, too, famous writer though she was, wanted to be alone," Max said, when they were under way, heading for the Mass. Turnpike. "I suppose, by an extension of the imagination, I can understand that. Solitude is comprehensible, though it has devastating effects upon one's conversation: have you ever noticed that the solitary, when they do see you, positively bubble over with talk, the pressure, no doubt, of all the ideas which have for so long gone unuttered?"

"That," Kate said, "is the disadvantage of truly rural solitude, which mine, you will have noticed, is not. That is, not constantly. I lose myself among the long grass and thickets only on occasional weekends, or on holidays from the university. But I know what you mean. Of course, those who work all day with many people can, if they have any gift for loneliness, use the evenings and weekends for periods of silence, the reordering, the rediscovery of experience. Such, I hope, is my way. But for those who are alone all day—as Cecily apparently was—I see there might be a problem."

"There are neighbors, of course, but they are mostly at some distance and, as is the way with this automobile culture, reachable only by car."

"You sound like me; but this automobile culture, as you call it, is taking you to where you want to be at this very moment."

"Only because there are no trains. Imagine, we might have taken a compartment, had tea served, or champagne, and watched the countryside flashing by to the reassuring click-clack of the wheels. No doubt about it, I was born a hundred years too late, in time to see all I might have treasured destroyed."

"Did Cecily feel that way, too? Odd, in that case, that she should have come to America at all."

"Cecily had two passions in her life: for Ricardo, her husband—one of her wilder eccentricities was always to call him by his last name—and for the sea. Once Ricardo died, there was only the sea. Her house is not, you know, quite on the sea, as are most in that part of the world. Hers is set back, across a meadow, so that the sea is visible from her windows, but the rocky coast is not; one must walk across the meadow in order to watch the waves crashing, in their implacable way, against the rocks. Her meadow," Max added with a certain stringency, "always had a neat path from her door to the sea mowed right through it. She couldn't live without the sea, but she said that, as in a good marriage, there must be both space and accessibility."

"Hooray for Cecily. Why have you only told me you knew her now she's dead?"

"Why, indeed. I saw little enough of her myself. She was a bit of a recluse in these last years, likely as not to forget one was coming, and give one a stale piece of cheese and a glass of wine for a meal. The wine, of course," Max added, with the air of one determined to be wholly reasonable, "was always excellent. She may have been miles from anywhere, up there in Maine, but in those elegant coastal parts there is money, and in so far as civilization can be bought, it is available."

23

With the sort of courtesy Kate always appreciated in Max, he fell silent as she executed the tricky by-pass of Boston, Revere, and several rotaries which seemed specifically designed to enable cars going in opposite directions to meet head-on. She was pleased to note, however, that she was almost alone in heading north: the other traffic was clearly looking for something more populated. Once safely on Route 1 leading to 95, she fell to thinking about Cecily Hutchins. Her death had come as a shock, partly because one had had no warning, no notice of disease or deterioration of spirit, but mostly because such a loss shook Kate's universe, which trembled in its furthest reaches. Cecily Hutchins had been one of those English authors who seem to escape, or avoid, the notice of reviewers or academic critics. She was too readable, perhaps; in the years before the seventies, too "feminine." One of those to whom the first crocus would always be a miracle. Fame, the sort that is marked by requests to appear on television talk shows and be photographed for the slicker magazines, had come to her late, when she had written a book about solitude, about her life alone on the rocky coast of Maine. But so firmly had she set herself against both the intrusive scholars and the blandishments of the media world that, eventually, these institutions had had to content themselves with tales of her marvelous, her mysterious privacy.

"Why do you think she went home to England to die?" Kate asked.

"I think death overtook her there," Max said. "She didn't go in search of it in England's green and pleasant land. What a romantic you are, Kate."

"She was well into her seventies. The possibility must

have occurred to her. Why not wait for death on the rocky coast you have loved?"

"I hope you are not considering taking up the authorship of Gothic novels. Could you have sought that primitive cabin for so nefarious a purpose?"

"Oh, rot. She continued to live on the coast of Maine full-time when Ricardo died, and could hardly bear to leave it even for a day; at least, that's what all the articles said. If suddenly she decided to visit England once again, there must have been a reason."

"None that was overpowering. Of course, her old dog had died, and she could go with an easier mind. Cecily, I regret to say, was one of those who willingly indenture themselves to representatives of the animal world, a regrettable but common English flaw. Also, if you want the most superficial excuse, she went to attend my nephew's wedding. But I don't for a moment think that was more than an excuse. She wanted to see England again, and happened to die there."

"You didn't attend your nephew's wedding?"

"Certainly not. I sent a gift erring only slightly on the side of extravagance, and went on about my business. After all, one cannot desert one's university post for transatlantic weddings, however familial. Besides, I would have had to fly madly back and forth, and I fly only when absolutely necessary. I was forgiven, my reputation for eccentricity and self-centeredness having by now established itself quite satisfactorily. Most people, dear Kate, err by trying to be thought generous, an ill-considered aim. Once you are thought selfish, not only are you forgiven a life designed mainly to suit yourself, which in anyone else would appear monstrous, but if an impulse to generosity should by chance overpower you, you will get five times the credit of some poor selfless soul who has been oozing kindness for years. Human beings must be carefully trained in what they can expect from you."

"I can't decide whether you're a quite sinister cynic, or merely Hal in *Henry the Fourth, Part One*."

"A distinction without a difference, my dear. 'Cynic' is the sentimentalist's name for the realist."

"Cecily seemed content to choose a realist for her literary executor, then. I should have thought an optimist would have been likelier to work to enhance her reputation."

"Cecily was an intelligent woman, and therefore a fatalist in these matters. Those who manufacture reputations are battling against the clock. Others, with faith in the eventual judgment of the ages, are content to be the foster child of silence and slow time. More to the point, I was the son of her best friend, and more suited than her own children in these literary matters. She gave them most of her money before she died anyway, and they'll get most of what's left now. I struggle alone with the papers and eventually a biography."

"Did she want a biography?"

"Not especially, but what good does that do one, with all the hungry academics and publishers buzzing around corpses these days? I, however, shall protect her. She knew she could count on me for that. And I'll do the biography she deserves."

"And what's in it for you, besides a lot of work?"

"Really, Kate, I'm not as wholly devoid of the ordinary human virtues as you might like to think. I simply don't prate on about them. I was fond of Cecily,

26

as was my mother. You need not make me out an ogre."

"Apologies. But you have said yourself the avoidance of personal burdens is one of your rules of life."

"Avoidance, not, as those horrible tax people say, evasion. I accept the duties that are properly mine. You are now saying to yourself, 'How unfeeling he is!' But I'm not, you know. I simply refuse to gush on in the accepted mindless way. Have you ever found me unresponsive to the claims of a friend and colleague?"

"No," Kate said, "I haven't. But then, having a pretty clear notion of your personality, I didn't make the claims excessive."

"My point exactly. Yet if, as might happen, I were the single person who could help you, would you not call upon me as I have called upon you, and would you not expect my compliance—my willing and gracious compliance?"

Kate stared at Max so long that, when her eyes returned to the road, she had to swerve the car rather wildly to get back in her lane. "Yes," she said. "You are right, Max. You are one of the people I trust and honor, and, what's more, have affection for, though I would not dream of coming to you if I merely required a shoulder on which to pour out my self-pity. I see your point; quite right, too."

They drove in silence for a certain time. "Of course," Kate said, after some miles, "I don't altogether understand what we hope to find on the rocky coast of Maine, or, at any rate, within the house."

"We hope to find everything in place, nothing out of the ordinary. I shall have to affirm that all her papers are in order, and ready to be moved out to whichever

27

famous library I decide to sell them to. But a visit was clearly necessary. Neighbors report prowlers, though not, I trust, accurately. Her children are just back from England and busy with their own affairs, having attended the wedding (and sent, I wager, a less extravagant present than I), and her lawyer began to make encouraging noises over the telephone. I thought of you to go with me, even before I knew I had to hunt you down in your mysterious retreat. You're not only a good driver, which I had hoped, you're a good conversationalist and good company, which I could count on. I envision a speedy but thorough examination of the house, a good dinner, a pleasant evening at the inn, and a pleasant ride back tomorrow to report that all is well. Whom do you think, by the way, I should approach about the papers? The Morgan, the Berg, Yale, Harvard, or the Wallingford? I lean toward the Wallingford myself, but on this subject, as on all others, I am open-minded. It is the Wallingford's reputation for intense discretion that inspires me."

"Hold on," Kate said. "We exit here. After this we will have to ask directions, I suppose."

"We shall. I have only been here a few times, and that not recently. I never could follow the dirt roads, complete with gates that have to be opened. Let's ask at the first service station."

two

The dirt roads were indeed complicated, dodging in and out of the woods, crossing one another, and affording occasional tantalizing glimpses of the sea. Max and Kate had been fortunate in finding an informed repairman refilling his gas tank at the service station where they had stopped to inquire, and Max, in his efficient way, made rapid notes as the complicated instructions were given. "You'll know when you've found the right road," the repairman said, "because there's a metal gate she's had put up. Not that it protected her from death," he philosophically added. "You have to get out, open it, get out again, close it, and after that . . . just keep going till the house is there."

Max opened the gate when, following the directions in his neat hand, they had reached it, waited for Kate to pull the car through, closed the gates again, and climbed back in for the final bit. "The gates, as I understand it, were to keep out casual sightseers, particularly in the summer, looking for the sea. Ah, there it is."

The house was certainly startling, perhaps, Kate asked herself, because something had led her to expect a turn-of-the-century mansion, surrounded by English roses? This house suggested that its architect might have submitted it for some contest in forward-looking design. Built of that sort of bleached wood that looks as though it had been deposited by the sea, the house had evidently been envisioned as standing upon the sea's edge looking as though it had been washed up there. When, Kate surmised, the architect had learned that his mad client wanted it set back across a meadow, he had not altered his design. Kate had never admired modern architecture as fervently as she had felt appropriate to someone of her advanced ideas, yet this house was exactly right to stand by the sea. Why had she supposed Cecily would want something with three floors and a central staircase?

Inside, the house was even more impressive, its large central room lit by the light from the sea, having in itself an aquatic quality as though it were part of an ocean kingdom. Only part of the house contained a second story, and here Cecily had reproduced the sort of room one might have found in an English manor house. The desk, the books, the carpet, the fireplace, the clutter of the room contrasted sharply with the clean lines of the central room below. So she had liked contrasts in her life. This room did not face the sea, as though one had to turn one's face from that vision while writing. Above the fireplace—it was the first thing to catch one's eye as one entered the room—was the portrait of a woman: young, blond, marvelously agreeable looking, and just not beautiful. Whoever she was, her chief characteristic had clearly been vitality— she looked like some sort of Scandinavian queen or female warrior, yet with laughter about it, as though she had appreciated the incongruity between her looks and herself. She was not laughing in the picture, but laughter was not far away, and when it came it would be at herself. I wonder who painted it, Kate thought first, and only after, I wonder who she is.

She asked Max, who had followed her slowly up the stairs, gazing about apprehensively. "No sign of prowlers," he said. "A mare's nest, no doubt. But I had better secure all the papers, while we are here. That?" he asked, remembering Kate's question. "The artist is more famous than the subject, which makes it a rather valuable portrait these days." He named the painter. "He was quite unknown, of course, when he painted it. The subject? She was named Whitmore. Dorothy Whitmore. Not a particularly impressive writer, who died young. She and Cecily were at Oxford together."

"But I've heard of her," Kate said. "In fact, one of my—"

"One does forget"—Max smiled—"that British literature of the last century and a half is your specialty."

"One of her novels was a great success; they even made a movie of it."

"Posthumously, alas, poor dear. Her will left all the receipts from her works to her Oxford college for scholarships, and the painting to my mother, who in turn left it to Cecily."

"Was your mother at Oxford, too?"

"Oh, yes. You see before you the son of one of the first Oxford women to get a degree. Not that my mother came all over academic, thank the Lord. One could only forgive one's mother for being a blue-stocking in her youth if she also had the intelligence to

31

marry the younger son of the younger son of a duke. Which, I am pleased to say, she did."

"Max, you are a snob—how enchanting of you in this day and age."

"Not a snob, dear, just selective, and no more so than some unwashed revolutionary who will associate only with his smelly kind. She kept her papers in here."

"In here" was a strictly utilitarian room, lined with fireproof cabinets. Max flung open one of these to reveal ordered files which contained, he explained to Kate, the correspondence of a long life as well as original drafts and manuscripts. All of these Cecily had retained believing, accurately, that they comprised a rare picture of her time.

"Odd," Kate said, "that she should have preserved everything so carefully, considering her love of privacy —the gate, the lonely house, all that. One would think a bonfire on the lawn, in the manner of Henry James and Dickens, would have been more in her line."

"I agree," Max said. "In fact, I have in the past done my best to persuade her of this. Her answer was oddly characteristic. 'Had I known,' she said to me, sitting downstairs in the main room, 'that this fetish for other people's mail would grow so widespread, I should have begun by destroying every letter after I had answered it. But to destroy them now would be to guarantee the preservation only of my side of every correspondence. I do not wish to impute any sinister motives to Dickens, or to James, whom I so much admire, but there must have been some satisfaction in removing forever from human sight that uncomfortable epistolary accusation, particularly since you know it to have been absolutely untrue.' I can remember her staring from the window out at the sea. 'You know, Max,' she said, 'I have lived in times of great change. The First World War, the early days of women's degrees at Oxford, the years between the wars when I knew, in various degrees of intimacy, the Bloomsbury group, writers like Rose Macaulay and Elizabeth Bowen, not to mention the whole peace movement. Lowes Dickinson and the hopes for the League. I have to recognize that this is an historical record, quite apart from any importance I may have had, and I am by no means ready to claim that I am of no importance. So the architect built me a file room, and I have preserved it all. You may want to burn it when I am dead, Max, but don't. Sell it for the best price you can get, and let the children spend the proceeds on installing an extra telephone to forestall the need to write letters and create all this evidence of a past age.' "

"Will the papers bring much?"

"Thirty thousand at least; more, if I am clever and persuasive. It will pay her children's telephone bills for life, however madly the telephone company continues to raise the rates. The next step, of course, is to get an appraiser up here. They come dear enough, God knows, but if you pick a good one, their word is as impeccable as that of the holy ghost. There'll be some wine here, I dare say. Shall we have a glass?"

This question, like most of Max's, was rhetorical, the flourish of ancient gallantry. He led the way to the small circular staircase which led back into the large, beautiful room. "Will you wait down there while I bring the wine?"

"Is there a loo up here?"

"Her bedroom and bath are off in that direction."

"That will be fine," Kate said. "I enjoy catching glimpses of her life. I'll join you in a moment."

Cecily's bedroom was the night retreat of a writer, reader, thinker. One recognized immediately the distinction between the bedroom of such a person and that of one whose bedroom had been "decorated." Largish night-tables stood on either side of the large bed—Kate suspected the old dog had shared it with her, in the last years. Books were still piled there, plus paper and pencil. The window faced east, intentionally, Kate was sure, so that the morning light flooded in and awakened the occupant early to another day. Living alone, she would have retired early at night, the life forces in the house retreating to this one room her spirit could fortify. Probably, sleeping less in later years, she had read into the night, the old dog snoring beside her.

"What utter rot," Kate snorted at herself, entering the bathroom and closing the door behind her. "For all I know, she retired at two in the morning with a bottle of gin and listened to rock music through earphones." But the silence had a quality which was that of order and of life arranged for the deployment of personal forces. Finishing with the bathroom, Kate wandered back into the study, sitting for a moment in Cecily's chair to stare at the portrait she herself must have seen every time she glanced up. Is it only one's imagination that those who die young are so vital in appearance? Kate had heard it said, perhaps only with the sort of truth which adheres to ancient superstition, that those who are to die young seem to sense it and to live with double the intensity and joy of others. A romantic theory, in both senses of the word.

The files in the next room would be worth a small

fortune to a budding scholar anxious to make a name, or, more literally, to a library prepared to purchase their contents. She pulled on one of the metal drawers, and was surprised, as she had been before with Max, to have it open; feeling a snooper, she closed it immediately. How odd that they weren't locked. But then, why, since she lived alone, should they be? Passing out again beneath the portrait of Dorothy Whitmore, Kate thought to herself: Here was a complete life, and, at the end, full of work and the sort of solitude which is true aloneness. Kate found herself envying this house by the sea, actually speculating, for a moment, if it might be for sale. What is it that, in middle age, made solitude so attractive? An English poet had expressed it in a verse that Kate, once having read, never forgot:

Beyond all this, the wish to be alone:
However the sky grows dark with invitation cards
However we follow the printed directions of sex
However the family is photographed under the flag-
    staff—
Beyond all this, the wish to be alone.

Never mind, Kate said to herself, unwinding down the circular stairs with one hand on the banister. My little cabin will have to do. Without the stimulation of the university, you would be chattering to yourself like a magpie within a week, Kate Fansler.

"The files are not locked," she said to Max, who was emerging from the kitchen with a tray.

"I know, more's the pity. One of the tasks I shall urge you to share with me is the discovery of a key. There must be one. We can't leave all this unlocked—

it's partly why I wanted to come. Of course," he added, pouring some white wine for Kate into a beautiful glass, "one can lock files easily enough by pressing a button, but one would like to anticipate opening them with something less dramatic than a blowtorch. To Cecily's papers," he added, raising his glass, "and to you for coming along and holding my hand. Bless you."

It was the nearest Max had ever come to a personal compliment, and Kate was pleased to acknowledge it. They sat for a time in the glow of the wine and that particular brightness of the afternoon just before the day begins to fade. Through the window they could see the sea, not crashing against the rocks, but beyond the coastline, calm, expansive, glittering—what Kate thought of as the optimists' view of the ocean.

Max appeared to echo her thoughts. "One ought to go to watch the waves crashing against the rocks to return oneself to the facts of earthly life," he said, putting down his wineglass with an air of finality. "Shall we go and walk about before the sun sets?"

"One of the reasons I spend my weekends guestless," Kate said, "is because it is always when I am feeling particularly lazy that someone suggests that exertion is unquestionably the next item on the day's agenda."

"Not here," Max said, reaching for the wine bottle. "You have been angelic to come this far. Never let it be said of me that I encouraged anyone to exercise. Why, I might endanger my reputation for fastidiousness, and you've no idea the years it has taken me to establish it."

Kate, laughing, rose to her feet. "Your reputation for all the virtues is still safe with me," she said. "In fact, safer. Who else but so fastidious and urbane a creature as yourself would require moral support on a visit to a house like this? Let us saunter to the sea, by all means. Does it," she asked as they left the house, "impose an emotional burden—this literary-executor business?"

"More than I would have anticipated, since you are so perspicacious as to ask," Max answered, lingering on the front stoop, or whatever the modern equivalent of the front stoop is. "I admired Cecily, and for me to admire is to go some way toward loving, as you have no doubt also gathered. You call me a snob, but I find it difficult to admire those I secretly scorn. That, if you want to know, is my definition of a liberal."

"The concept of 'liberal,' like the concept of goodness, must have some hidden force behind it; it inspires so many people to disdain. Never mind," Kate said, her mind upon the mowed path to the sea, which was, indeed, a good idea, particularly if one thought of her overgrown meadow. But there—clever Cecily—the path led from her to the sea, not, obviously, from anywhere to her. Max, following her gaze, misapprehended her thoughts.

"It is unusual to have this much land near the sea," he said. "This house and the land around it is probably Cecily's most valuable bequest to her children. I believe that there are other houses visible on the coast, but considering the land's value, she was wonderfully isolated. Shall we follow the path to the sea, or explore the woods behind?"

"Oh, the sea, of course," Kate said, preceding him down the steps from the front modern-version-of-a-stoop and onto the path. It was not quite wide enough for two to walk abreast, and Kate led the way. The walk to the sea was not long, and Kate was shocked at how abruptly the land ended. Below it there was a drop to the rocks below, although a stairway of rocks had been cut to aid the descent of any intrepid soul.

"Let's go down," Kate said.

"Don't be impulsive," Max answered. "One of us— and it would no doubt be me—might break a leg and require rescue, which, from here, looks impossible. The other would have to stand by, teetering on a rock, and watch the tide come in, to our certain destruction. With what force the waves crash out there! Let's admire it from here, like the lady and gentleman we are. Do you suppose it's high tide or low?"

"Low, I should deduce," Kate said, "not that I know a thing about tides. But those pools there, between the higher rocks, must have got water into them, and yet water isn't going in now."

"Perhaps it's rain water."

"Look here, Max, I'm going down. After all, there *are* steps, and they wouldn't have been put there only for the purposes of suicide. I should like to watch the water crashing against the rocks close up. You watch if you are as timid as all that, and if I appear on the verge of destruction, you can go for help."

"But I can't drive. Really, Kate."

"You can use the telephone. Your entire charm, Max, is your unflappableness. No bachelor should come all over mother hen. It spoils the whole style. Fortunately I am wearing pants and crepe-soled shoes, another example of the serendipity of all this. I always wear very ladylike shoes when I know I am going to meet you."

In fact, Kate soon decided, scrambling over the rocks, the whole little scene had been nonsense. There

38

was no real danger except, she supposed, of slipping and breaking a leg. One simply leaped relatively short distances from one rock to the next. At one of the higher points, Kate paused. The waves dashing against the rocks *were* impressive, not to say a bit daunting. She resisted an impulse to dash back across the rocks to dry land and nature's more controllable forces. But she did turn around and noticed, then, in a pool between two rocks rather to her right, what looked like a bundle of clothes.

She became aware, as one does after a shock, of a plunging sensation in her stomach, which had received the message of disaster seconds before her conscious mind. With the summoning of all her determination, Kate forced herself nearer to the pool. For a moment she looked back for Max, and was astonished to discover she could not see him. She could see only rocks. Reaching a rock nearer to the pool, Kate sat upon it and waited for her pulse to stop racing. Then she looked down. It was a body, a woman's body, face down in the pool. Each time the sea came in, a slight spray spattered it.

Responding to a sudden surge of adrenalin, which, we are told, is what rushes into our bloodstream to provide the flight or fight reaction necessary to survival, Kate leaped back with abandon over the rocks, and then found she had lost track of the stairs. "Max," she shouted. "Max."

Max, coming nearer to the edge, peered down at her. "All adventurous spirits properly subdued?" he asked. "You can't get up this way, you know. The stairs are over there." He gestured to his left. Again Kate leaped over the rocks and this time up the stairs.

39

"Max," she said. "There's a body down there. A woman's body."

If some witty rejoinder occurred to Max, he controlled it at the sight of her face. "Are you sure?"

"We had better go for help."

"Would it not be more sensible to telephone?"

"Of course. I'm upset."

"No you're not. The telephone's been disconnected. We had better go for help. Come on."

"Don't you think," Kate said, "that you had better wait here until I return with whatever rescue I can collect?"

"What on earth for? No one's likely to bother the body. It may have been there for days, for all you know. Or weeks."

"Suppose the tide comes in."

"I, my dear lady, cannot stop the tides. Perhaps I ought to see if I can find you some whisky or brandy in the house."

"No, I have to drive. For God's sake, Max, come on!"

three

Hours later, or days, or weeks (but was it perhaps only minutes?), Kate and Max, in the back of a police car, were being driven from Cecily's house to the police station. Kate's own car, which, she supposed, they had or were about to search for signs of God knew what, followed under the guidance of a young police officer. One might, of course, look at one's watch. Kate looked at her watch. Perhaps two hours had passed since she had clambered down the rocks like some blasted mountain goat, instead of remaining with Max on the shore as any respectable middle-aged professor of English literature ought to be counted on to do.

Kate and Max had returned with the police, and several of them had bounded out to discover if they had come for a practical joke, a rescue operation, or an hallucination; they had returned to report, yes indeed, a body, and would the lady and gentleman mind waiting up at the house until the body was recovered and they might all make their decorous way to the police station? The waiting time had been occupied with questions from a policeman, none of which appeared to be answered to his satisfaction. Who Max was he easily established, but no fact after that made any

41

sense, at least to a laconic, unimaginative policeman born and bred in a small town in Maine. They had come on an impulse? There was no relationship between them; they were friends and colleagues? A likely story, his entire manner implied. They had not come with any particular purpose in mind, but simply to look around and search for a key to the files? News of prowlers? The police had heard none of this, and if not the police, who? What neighbors? Had they found the key to the files? Oh, they had decided to look at the sea before searching the house? Did they expect to find the key washed up by the sea? The sarcasm and doubts had been more implied than expressed, but Kate's imagination was working at full force, and little more than a raised eyebrow was needed to set it off.

Max, meanwhile, had turned into a bundle of self-incrimination. He ought never to have come, never to have brought her; he, Max Reston, had behaved impulsively and look what had happened. One could almost turn the whole episode into a cautionary tale. That Max, for whom forethought and rationality were second nature, should have acted like a student rebel was more dreadful than he could say. Nonetheless, he said it. Still, being Max, he did not wallow in regret, but set himself to calming Kate and urging upon her a brandy or another glass of the excellent wine. Never mind what the policeman thinks, Max had said, he was doubtless already assured that they were reprehensible people, but would learn with whom he was dealing at the proper time. Meanwhile, one could only do one's best to regain one's equilibrium. Under Max's ministrations, Kate partly did.

They arrived at the police station, and Kate was

permitted to call Reed. He, having suggested that she reveal to the police his, Reed's, connection with the district attorney's office, and having offered to come to her rescue, ended by talking with someone at the station and establishing that she and Max would be permitted to drive to Logan Airport in Boston and fly from there to New York. All of this, when it was finally sorted out, did help to clear the atmosphere somewhat. The police, whether gladly or reluctantly, faced the fact that they were dealing not with hippies, a love nest, or a pack of middle-aged perverts engaged in sodomy, but two perfectly respectable people who had every right to be where they were, who had found a body and immediately reported it, in the most correct possible manner, to the police.

"There is only one other thing," announced the chief policeman, whose manner had become as cordial as his expressionless voice and face permitted. "Before you leave, I must ask you to look at the body. It will not be pleasant, since it has been in the water some time, perhaps several days. We will know after the autopsy. But if either of you recognize the young woman—perhaps a friend of Miss Hutchins?" he added hopefully to Max, "—we would be helped along a good bit."

"This," Max said quietly to Kate, as they followed the chief to the lower reaches of the building, "is where breeding shows. We will brace ourselves, carry it all through with aplomb, express no more emotion than is absolutely appropriate, and take it out in our dreams."

"How could we possibly know her?" Kate asked.

"A good point." Max stopped in the corridor. "Sir," he called to the man walking ahead of him. "There is, of course, a chance that I might recognize the body as

43

some connection of Miss Hutchins, though that seems unlikely. But there is no way Miss Fansler could recognize the body, since she has never been near here until today. Might we not spare her this ordeal?"

"Routine," was the only answer.

In fact, they were as considerate of Max and Kate as the circumstances permitted. The body was drawn out in a kind of drawer in which it lay, covered and refrigerated. The covering was lowered only far enough to reveal the face, which, the man explained, had been "cleaned up." "In her early twenties," the chief said. "That might help to place her."

Kate braced herself, and Max placed a hand on her near shoulder in support. Ever after Kate was to remember her feeling of relief that the face, however horrible, looked less horrible than she had expected. She immediately recognized it. The recognition seemed a touch of sanity for one blinding moment, until her brain registered the fact that the young woman before her was dead, and had been dead for several days.

"I do know her," Kate said. "She's a student of mine. A graduate student. Her name is Marston; Geraldine Marston, called Gerry by her friends. . . ."

"Fine," the policeman shot out in a loud voice. He's right, Kate thought, I was beginning to babble. "Let's go back upstairs. Boyd, get some brandy for the lady. This way, please." The drawer was pushed back in, and the policeman took Kate's arm and guided her back upstairs and into a chair. "Drink this," he said. Boyd, Kate thought, must be a rapid fellow. Gerry Marston!

In the end, it was decided that Max would be asked to stay, since he had at the moment the nearest thing to legal jurisdiction over the house. A policeman would drive Kate to Logan Airport and hand her over to her husband, who was at this moment flying to Boston. He, the policeman, supposed that a husband would be comforting even to a woman who did not care to use his name. If he was her husband. They drove in silence, Kate because she was afraid to speak at all for fear, as one of her colleagues put it with more accuracy than elegance, of running off at the mouth, and the policeman because he was Maine enough to consider conversation with strangers best avoided.

Sitting in the airplane by Reed's side, however, sipping a vodka martini, Kate felt she could trust herself to speak. Instead, of course, she started to cry, not noisily, but with the tears streaming down her face. "Never mind," Reed said, producing a large handkerchief. "Cry away. No, the stewardess will not think you are drunk, only bereaved. Perhaps she will decide I have told you of my passion for another woman, and you are trying to persuade me not to break up our happy home. That's better. A faint smile, but a smile, indubitably."

"I keep thinking about her, and remembering her. I would never have believed I could remember her so clearly, in such detail, or that my conversations with her would seem so vivid. That, no doubt, is what the poets keep telling us about life—we never perceive it with intensity until someone has drowned in a rocky pool. At least, that's what poets used to tell us, before they abandoned intensity and syntax altogether. I sound like a congressman from the Middle West, of a particularly conservative persuasion. But, Reed, what can she have been doing there? Was she, who *was* from the Middle West, overcome with a need to see the sea? Surely she can't have been robbing Cecily—not of the silver, I mean, but of papers and so on? She didn't seem that sort. And why should she have decided to go rock climbing? Why did I, if it comes to that? Could her body have been thrown there?"

"Let's not speculate until after the autopsy. I gather Max did not recognize her?"

"No. Why on earth should he?"

"Well, she had been at the university. He might have passed her on the campus."

"I'm sure Max never noticed anyone to whom he hadn't been properly introduced, certainly not one of the thousands of graduate students swarming about the place. She was a nice girl, Reed—what an old-fashioned phrase that is. An old-fashioned nice girl, and holding down a job to stay in school, though she had some sort of fellowship to pay her tuition. Her parents were poor; the whole heart-rending bit. I hope to God she was not their only child, but I have a sinking feeling that she was. Why should the thought that she was not, Reed, make it any easier to bear? Tell me that."

"There will be nothing easy about this news," Reed said. "Someone is on the way to deliver it now, miles away, even in another time zone. Kate, you have got to pull yourself together sufficiently to realize how absolutely extraordinary your whole story is. I don't blame the Maine police for deciding you and Max were involved in dark and nefarious sin; how not, under the circumstances? When Max told me he was going to seek you out, I'm afraid I barely listened; more's the pity. I should have told him you were addressing a group of gay activists in Minneapolis. That would have scared him off."

46

"I expect Max was nervous being left with the results of Cecily's death. After all, the decision not to marry or involve oneself in anothers' life is supposed to be insurance against just this sort of thing. I think it touching that Max wanted his hand held, and by the least motherly female around."

Reed reached over and opened the second little bottle of vodka martini provided by the airline; he poured it into Kate's glass and stirred it for her. "You do realize, my darling, why it may have had to be you who accompanied Max on this touching mission? Because you could identify the body for him and get any suspicion nicely turned in another direction."

Kate swallowed this statement with the first sip of her second martini. Then she shook her head. "Too clever by half," she said. "You are, I am to gather, suggesting that Max, having got the body into the pool, wanted it identified by someone suspicious. But, Reed, if he had been responsible for that body, which is ridiculous on the face of it, the last thing he would want is any connection with it at all. Besides, what could he possibly accomplish by dragging me up there to identify the body? Whenever it died, I was nowhere near Maine, and could certainly prove it. But you know, there is a connection, not between Max and Gerry, but between Gerry and the house. Of course. That portrait. She was doing her dissertation on Dorothy Whitmore, and wanted, perhaps, to see the painting. It is extraordinary, that portrait. That's why she was there, Reed; that has to be why she was there. That, or hoping for Whitmore papers, though she didn't strike me as a snooper in the least."

"No doubt you're right. And at a less elevated

47

moment, you must tell me about Dorothy Whitmore, Cecily Hutchins, and the story of English women novelists of the past century. Meanwhile, it would seem, if your speculation is accurate, that she was discovered by someone who may well have been after the silver, enticed or bullied onto the rocks, and killed. The police will have to find that prowler. He must have been fairly vigorous, for starters."

"Or seductive."

"I thought you said she was a nice girl, old-fashioned and all that?"

"Exactly why he would have had to be seductive, in a subtle way," Kate said, feeling a bit better. But the pain of Gerry's death had taken hold, and would never entirely abate.

In the weeks that followed, the police in Maine came, apparently, to the same conclusion as had Reed and Kate in the plane. They set about discovering the prowler, and were somewhat helped in this by the date of death, surprisingly established within a day or two by the medical experts. The girl had drowned, having first been hit on the head or, more probably, having hit her head on a rock after slipping. She had died, expert opinion was as certain as expert opinion ever allows itself officially to be, not less than three, not more than five days before the body was found. High tide and rough seas had dashed the body against the rocks as it lay in the small pool, but these injuries, received after death, were so identified. She was in good health—no disease of any sort to suggest another cause of death. And yes, of course, it was perfectly possible that she had died alone and by accident. Surely she would have

48

been foolish to climb out on those rocks when no one knew she was going, or would realize that she was gone, but having done so, she might well have slipped, hit her head, fallen forward into the pool, and drowned. Altogether unsatisfactory, but where there was no motive, it seemed foolish to suggest murder. An unfortunate accident. Signs warning visitors away from the coast were suggested, but the residents pointed out, as they had before, that the coast hereabouts was private, and trespassers—this was not quite said—deserved what they got.

And that, it appeared, was that. The prowler was not discovered, despite profound questioning of everyone who might have seen such a person. No one had seen anyone. How, then, had Maximillian Reston come to hear of a prowler? This question, too, innocently resolved itself. An old lady with a house on the same private road had been for her afternoon constitutional, and walking up near Cecily's house—they had been friends, and this was an established custom the old lady saw no reason now to change—she had seen a man about the place. No, she could not really tell anything about him. But she felt it her duty to let Max know. She was in her late seventies, and while vigorous, as lonely and eccentric (the police used another word unofficially) as Cecily. Max responded to this warning because he felt guilty about the papers. Since the old lady had also been in touch with Cecily's lawyer, an old-time resident of the town whom she knew well, additional pressure had been put on Max to cope. It all fitted in neatly, and bit by bit the case faded away.

As for Kate Fansler, who agreed, in that entirely improper way, to accompany a man to Maine and spend

49

the night with him in a local inn, she was absolutely and indisputably elsewhere at the time of the death, however widely one extended this. The police clearly, if inaudibly, were regretful. She would have made a nice solution. But at all the days and hours when Geraldine Marston might have died, Kate Fansler, who turned out to be a rather well-known professor of English at a prominent university with all sorts of important connections, was holding forth (one gathered she did rather hold forth) in the presence of several people at the least, except at night, when her husband, whose qualifications were awe-inspiring, even in Maine, was prepared to swear that she was with him.

There for several months the matter rested. It was not until late March that the thought of Geraldine Marston became again, for Kate, more than a dull, persistent pain and a sad memory.

four

The elevator opened directly into the gymnasium, disgorging its occupants into what would certainly have been one of the circles of hell had Dante been prescient enough to have thought of it. Fortunately for him and the world of medieval literature, he had lived too soon to envision the ambiance of the gymnasium of an all-male school in the last third of the twentieth century. Kate Fansler, whom experience seemed incapable of preparing for the assault on her senses, paused to allow herself to regain what equanimity the scene allowed. It wasn't much. The smell of twenty-five or more adolescent male bodies engaged in relentless athletics, while at first apparently beyond the bounds of adult human endurance, would, Kate knew from experience, be reduced by the blessed action of olfactory fatigue. The noise, emanating in the main from a loudspeaker system amplifying the latest rock at several decibels above that safe for human hearing, would subside, not, as seemed likely, from the deafness of the spectators, but from the beginning of the game, when the speaker system would be blessedly shut off. "But what," Kate had asked her nephew Leo, "can be the point of that awful noise, that deafening cacophony?"

"We like it." Leo was by now inured to his aunt's tendency toward polysyllabic expression. "Besides," he conceded in the interests of truth, "it psychs up the team."

"My God," Kate had answered. She was capable of monosyllables when shocked.

The noise from the loudspeaker system did not quite drown out the other sounds from the gymnasium—the screams of young males, varying from bass to soprano in range, but remarkably similar in tone and vocabulary; the bells and ancient car horns being practiced for subsequent use in the expression of joy at a basket, home team or not, as the case might be.

Having taken account of smell and sound, Kate turned to consider the next feat required of her: the climb, through obdurately unmoving male bodies, up the grandstand to a seat from which she might watch the game. A backless seat, of course, providing little foot room and no place for one's coat and other accouterments: Kate had learned to limit these, and to wear only pantsuits to the gymnasium. One evening of tugging helplessly at her skirts had been enough.

"Hi, Kate!" John Crackthorne's mature tones managed somehow to make themselves heard. He patted a place next to him, and Kate, waving wildly in recognition—for no lesser gestures would have been observable—began the search for footholds between the stolid bodies of small boys.

"Hey, you, Alderman, Watson, Levy, let the lady up, please." Crackthorne accompanied this command with certain well-placed kicks and blows. The boys addressed, suddenly awakened to their roles of courteous youths, as opposed to athletic demons, arose, revealing ties, blazers, and the promise of civilization, and let Kate pass.

"Marvelous to see you," Crackthorne said. "You are becoming one of our most faithful followers of the team. Is it vicarious pleasure or support of your nephew? Direct pleasure it can scarcely be, so I don't suggest it."

"Leo *seems* to like me to come," Kate answered. "Of course, he never asks me or notices me while I'm here. But he does announce when the game will be, and I have observed that all the others starters have faithful parents who attend with touching regularity. When I ask Leo if I should come, he always says, 'If you feel like it, it's O.K.,' which, translated, means: I would like to have you there, but I would rather feel that you had insisted upon coming over my demurrings. The translation may, of course, as translations so often are, be distorted by the preconceptions of the translator. Why do you attend so faithfully?"

"All five boys are in my English class, and by coming I gain a certain moral ascendance over the basketball coach. He tried to retaliate by attending my English classes, but couldn't fit it in between practices; the one time he came he fell asleep. Alas, so often, do the boys, from too much basketball practice—but you don't want to hear any more of our tedious school wrangles. I understand if we win tonight, we can scarcely fail to have an undefeated season, a fact which the boys and I partly regret. Why has it never occurred to anyone that God, if he existed, would clearly be seen to be regularly on the wrong, if winning, side? We ought to have lost gracefully, while gaining school fame with a

53

smashing performance by the orchestra or dramatic society. But such is not life."

Anyone watching them, Kate supposed, would assume them to be involved in a relationship of great intimacy. Through long practice, Kate and Crackthorne had discovered that if one put one's mouth exactly as though one were about to kiss the ear of the other, words might actually be exchanged. To any visitor from Mars—who, however, if he were clever enough to get to earth, would be smart enough not to enter the gymnasium—it would appear that Kate and Crackthorne derived great pleasure from the lengthy kissing of one another's ears.

"Ah," Kate said. She by now knew the signs. The teams left the floor, either for last-minute instructions in their locker room or, as Kate rather suspected, to enable them to make an entrance in their handsome warm-up suits. Kate had learned from Leo that no uniform was too fine for varsity teams, though the science teacher had been heard muttering about the shortage of Bunsen burners, and the library, however elegant, could certainly have done with some judicious filling in.

Kate, under Leo's relentless instruction, delivered for the most part as an accompaniment to televised Knick games, had become something of a basketball aficionado. To her own and Leo's regret, she could never recognize when someone had set a "pick," and she tended to admire the wrong members of any team she watched; also, her most regrettable failing from Leo's point of view, she disapproved staunchly of the Wilt Chamberlain type, all those over seven feet tall. She maintained that the game should be limited to those

54

six feet five or under, and no amount of explanation on Leo's part of the grace and talent of these tall men could reconcile Kate to the unfair advantage of their height. Still, Leo forgave her these failings because she maintained both her interest and a knowledge of her ignorance; those elders who pretended to understand the game when they did not, which was mostly, were the scorn of the boys. Similarly, if Leo should want to know something about a work of literature for an exam, whose imminence always coincided with his first reading of the work to be examined, he would wander into Kate's room and say: "Let's hear a few bright remarks about 'Prufrock.'" Kate rather admired this mutual exchange of needed information, made possible by her willingness to leave the initiation of all conversations to Leo. Those conversations whose nature required they be initiated elsewhere, Kate, with great cowardice, left to Reed. The system worked surprisingly well.

It was Leo's parents' unwillingness to leave any initiative at all to Leo that had shattered, once and for all, Leo's ability to get along with them or even, eventually, to remain in the same house. Whether because he was the middle son of three, or because of odd personality clashes, or because, in Kate's opinion, her brother was a stuffed shirt with a closed mind and her sister-in-law a beautifully dressed and coiffured busybody with no mind at all, Leo had needed to escape. Once before in his life he had turned up, so to speak, on Kate's doorstep and lived with her for a summer. Now, in his senior year in high school, he was living with her again. Reed had agreed they would try it, and it had worked, not that either Kate or Reed deluded themselves about the reasons. First, their apartment was large; second, they had ample domestic help; third, they were able to maintain an indifference to Leo's actions which, such is the perversity of adolescence, impelled him to discuss them and thus allow a certain degree of guidance; fourth, and most important, Leo wanted to get on with Kate and Reed, the alternatives being to live with his parents, which was unthinkable, or go to boarding school, which was undesirable.

It had, of course, been left to Kate once again to soothe the ruffled ego of her brother. He had argued with his eldest about the Vietnam war, alienated his second son, and seemed to suspect Kate, unladylike enough not to have produced any progeny of her own, of eyeing the third, Ted, now in the eighth grade. But Kate had been able to assure him that many adolescents like Leo were better off not living at home and boarded out, which was certainly true, and that Ted, the third son, already able to flatter his father into too large an allowance, was at thirteen too far down the primrose path for Kate to offer him house room should he want it. Sometimes, at the basketball games, Kate tried to picture her brother and sister-in-law watching, and failed wholly in this imaginative effort. "Some of us," Kate had said to Reed, "were born to be aunts and uncles. A valuable and underrated role."

"Still," Reed had answered, "the roles might have been easier could you have managed to latch on to an uncoordinated nephew five feet six or, better still, a niece. One can grow tired of basketball."

"It intrigues me," Kate had said. And Leo was content to discuss other things with Reed. It made for pleasantness all around.

With a great whoop, mercifully accompanied by the

cessation of the rock music, the teams returned. The starters doffed their warm-up regalia, and the loud-speaker began announcing the teams. As each name was announced, its owner rushed out to the court and stood there, avoiding all eyes. When the teams were assembled, the captains shook hands—Kate, watching this grudging gesture, was reminded that hand-shaking supposedly derived from an examination of the other man's sleeve for hidden weapons—and the centers crouched to await the jump.

It was at this point that Kate and Crackthorne, their eyes upon the game, customarily began a discussion of literature, or gossip of the school or university. Kate had once attended a game without Mr. Crackthorne and had found it almost dull. She did not, of course, tell this to Leo. Crackthorne had been a student of Kate's some years back, having completed all the work for his Ph.D. save the dissertation, which, in a fashion all too familiar to Kate, seemed to be dragging on over the years. To support himself he had come to St. Anthony's to teach English. This year, however, he had begun to speak as though, with a certain amount of application in the coming summer, he might actually hope for the completion of what Kate believed would be a first-rate piece of work on those writers of the World War I generation in English who had survived.

She said as much to him, watching, out of the corner of her eye, the team's ball handler dribble down the court with one hand while signaling plays with the other. One of Kate's special delights in basketball arose from the analogy, for her, of the ball handler on the team and her own work in seminars, an analogy which earned only a snort from Leo, who considered Kate too prone to analogies anyhow.

"I am plunged in gloom," Crackthorne said. "It is like trying to stuff a pillow into a case too small for it. Everything keeps lapping over. Of course, these English types all knew one another, so that one is forever following some trail which leads to new wonders. Meanwhile, what I have written seems tedious beyond words."

"Inevitable," Kate said. "That's because you are so familiar with what you have that you assume it must be boringly familiar to everyone else. But it isn't. Snip off the edge of the pillow, cram the feathers into what's left of the case, sew up the edge as neatly as you can, and *then* think about other delightful paths down which you might be led. Beautiful shot! Hooray for Leo! You take my point, I trust, although basketball has a distinctly deleterious effect on my syntax and similes."

Kate, with an eye on the electric scoreboard, realized that the quarter was ending and that the chances of St. Anthony's having an undefeated season were good. As the end-of-the-quarter whistle blew, Crackthorne turned to Kate and began a discussion of Aldous Huxley, who, now he came to think of it, would have been in his youth an interesting prospect to an American coach, had he had decent eyesight and the misfortune to be born in the U.S. For a moment Kate tried to picture Huxley torn between basketball and the creation of *Crome Yellow*. She said as much to Crackthorne.

"Any of those English," he said, with one eye on the court as the second quarter began. "In my wilder moments, I try to imagine the coach inducing coordination in Lytton Strachey. *There*'s someone who would have managed to puncture all this nonsense. The coach, as you might guess, dismisses all modern English writers of my period as pansies. I told him the word was buggers, but he thinks buggers were those employed by the Nixon administration. Speaking of Huxley, have you heard about the time . . ."

During the half, when the rock music resumed and the team disappeared, Kate and Crackthorne went downstairs to have a smoke and a little relative quiet. St. Anthony's was leading by 34 points, which seemed to shed upon the rest of the evening a certain air of anticlimax; but Leo had warned her how often the Knicks had come back to win in the fourth quarter. Desertion was not, therefore, to be thought of.

As Crackthorne and Kate prepared to ascend to the inferno they were intercepted by Mr. Kunstler, the assistant coach, who was in charge of the junior varsity and remedial reading. With the ebullience inevitable in one able to follow such a career, he greeted Crackthorne with excited praise about how well his eggheads were doing on the basketball court and, upon being introduced to Kate, broke into little spurts of delight at the mention of her name.

"How proud you must be of your son, Mrs. Fansler. Leo gives some of the coaches a hard time, but I say he's a good boy and shows the results of a mother's loving care. One can always—"

"Kunstler, old boy—" Crackthorne began.

"I know it is no longer fashionable to praise motherhood," Kunstler continued, raising an admonishing hand, "but one can always spot the boys who have had a true mother's devotion. Some of our boys—"

"Kunstler, old chap, *shut up*. This is *Miss* Fansler, Leo's aunt, and she has never been a mother. If I were you, I would take my theories of motherhood and——"

"Well, well," Kunstler responded with marvelous sangfroid, "a fine boy, even if his mother is dead. You have nobly stepped into her place." Since there seemed no sane response to this but a formal bow, Kate bowed formally and allowed Crackthorne to lead her rather suddenly into the elevator, leaving Kunstler several paces behind as the door closed; doubtless he was still rapt in thoughts of devotion to motherhood.

But just as the elevator door was about to close, an arm, interfering, caused it to reopen. Six extremely large noisy boys occupied the elevator, as an invading army occupies a country, diminishing, belittling all other people and occupations and ways of life. There welled up in Kate a feeling of resentment against the young, already initiated male that nothing in years of sophistication or accomplishment had managed to still. They strutted; their self-absorption was absolute, their arrogance of status palpable. Crackthorne, if he did not share Kate's visceral response, deplored the dissipation within the elevator's enclosed atmosphere of a machismo indifference to all who were neither young nor masculine.

"Ricardo," Crackthorne snapped. "Might we at least mimic, if we cannot experience, some consideration for others. This is an elevator, not a beer hall." The door at that moment opened again upon the gymnasium, upon noise, rock music, and male sweat. But Kate moved gratefully from, as it were, condensed to diluted adolescence. Crackthorne caught up with her after a few more words to the invaders. Suddenly, the name he had snapped out in the elevator registered in her mind. "Ricardo?" she asked.

Crackthorne led the way up the grandstand, finding, and reserving for her use, footholds in the rows of boys.

"Chet Ricardo," he said when they were seated. "One of the cool set. You know, women, drugs, and a general air of smoothness at age fifteen. By senior year they're revealed as not terribly bright, having peaked too early. Leo, I am pleased to say, is not among them."

"Any relation to the painter Ricardo?"

"But of course, I should have realized why you wondered. Yes indeed, grandson, and of the famous Cecily Hutchins, which is more to the point for you and me. Papa is, alas, a rather uninteresting businessman: the genes are lying low until at least the fourth generation, or so it would seem."

"Funny Leo never mentioned him."

"My dear madam, no class graduates but the parents say, 'I was so *astonished* when sonny boy brought home his yearbook: there were at least *ten boys* I'd never *heard* of.'"

Not for the first time Kate pondered the strange habits of the young. In adolescence, the search for identity took many forms, most of them hideous. "Do you know," she bellowed into Crackthorne's ear, "I think we may safely consider this game won and our duty to the athletic young performed. I see they are taking out Leo and friends and putting in the second team. May I buy you a drink in the relative quiet of a singles bar, that being all the neighborhood affords?"

"No," he said. "I'll see it through and have some

encouraging words for those on the second team who will now trip all over their feet, miss the great chance of which they have been dreaming, and need to be comforted in their discovery of the distance between hope of performance and performance."

"I suspect you of being a born schoolteacher," Kate said, "something apparently rarer in our day than a fine glass blower, and infinitely more desirable. Until our next victory, then."

Later that evening Kate knocked on the door of her husband's study and, on being commanded to enter, stuck in her head. "Busy?" she asked.

"Longing to be distracted. It is the end of March, and my thoughts turn inevitably taxward. Yet, I say to myself, I may be run over tomorrow, and what a pity to have started so soon."

"If you are run over, how much easier for me to have all your financial affairs neatly in shape."

"Unfeeling woman. What is it, Kate? I thought you were writing a speech which had to be at least forty minutes long, even allowing for a generous question period."

"I was thinking of a classmate of Leo's I encountered today. It was a one-way meeting; he did not encounter me, unless a tank can be said to encounter the weed in its path. May I lounge in that Swedish leather thing with the machinery?"

"Lounge away." Reed leaned back in his swivel desk chair, and rested his feet on an open desk drawer. Kate noticed that no flesh appeared between trouser and sock.

"I keep being reminded of that day with Max," Kate said.

"The tank reminded you? Kate, I've been meaning to ask, have you ever thought of coaching a female basketball team? You must be damned well qualified by now, ready to tell them they should be able to dribble with either hand without watching the ball. Not so different from teaching English, really."

"Reed, I do love you. When is one of us going to start feeling tied up and run for life?"

"Never, is my plan. I not, because tied up is exactly what I want to feel. You not, because I mean to give you so much space to move about in you'll begin to miss me and seek me out."

"As I do now. Admirable man—and the house in the woods has helped. Reed, I'm the most fortunate person alive, and every now and then I've the feeling it's all a charade, and if I stop, there will be the pain."

"It's hard to be happy, and safe, and applauded in a miserable world. What *was* it about the boy in the elevator?"

"He seemed like nemesis, or destiny, or just my troubled conscience. Oh, I don't mean the boy himself, frightful male adolescent, than which, of course, when it is bad there is nothing worse. I just mean Cecily Hutchins, and Dorothy Whitmore, and Gerry Marston. I wonder where her portrait is now, and whether Max did sell the papers to the Wallingford."

"Why not have him to lunch at the Cos Club and ask him?"

"Reed, did I say I loved you?"

"Twice," Reed said, leaning over the desk and reaching out his hand.

part two

{ *April* }

five

It was, however, near the end of April before Max and Kate could arrange for a luncheon. Max was supposedly deep into the affairs of Cecily. As for Kate, commitments, speeches she had (in the calmer autumn months) agreed to make, were almost upon her; uncorrected proofs, unread manuscripts, unanswered letters piled up on her desk. At the university, all the crises, as inevitable in April as daffodils and forsythia, bloomed: next year's budget, catalogue, staff, this year's dissertations, exams, collapses. In the midst of all this, Reed and Kate were caught up, in loco parentis as they were to Leo, in the great college climax, the end of all the schools' endeavors for success of the kind that matters: letters were received from colleges, saying who had been accepted where. Kate and Reed, not especially astonished to learn that Leo had got into Harvard, where his male relatives had ever gone, were somewhat more so to be told that he intended to go, not to Harvard, but to Swarthmore. Leo's father was heard from. Kate went off, grumbling, to a luncheon at Fraunces Tavern with her brother, who refused to accept the news that his son had to be left to make his own decisions without at least berating his sister, whose fault, obviously, all this was. Kate, drowning her distaste in cool white wine, of which she had ordered a large bottle, thought he had better rave at her than at Leo.

That behind her, Kate returned to her cluttered desk. But Leo, it soon developed, was involved not only in his own college choice, but in that of all his classmates (save the ten unheard-of ones mentioned by Crackthorne), among whom, it soon transpired, Ricardo no longer was.

"*He* got into Harvard," Leo reported in disgust.

"He has very famous grandparents."

Leo's answer to this was a one-syllable expletive, the repetition of which, Kate promised, would end the conversation for a week. But Leo was truly disturbed.

"The guy's a creep. Everyone knows that. Frank told him he couldn't possibly get into Harvard. He's never worked in his life."

Frank was the college counselor at the school, a man so adept at dealing with admissions offices at colleges that he knew where each boy would be accepted weeks before the April 15 date. Indeed, Kate, watching the process, felt his talents to be wasted on this: surely a foundation or government bureau could have better used them. But for such a school, college acceptance stood at the very peak of its values, and however weak the members of the faculty, or the administration, the strength of personality was here, where it was needed. Kate, who had met Frank more than once, admired him, as she admired anyone who did his job well. She understood, furthermore, that Frank, however committed to Madison Avenue techniques, did not lie. He knew a lie to a college would only backfire in years to come. When he said, this year, to Yale: "You must take ten boys because they are all first-rate," they trusted him because the year before, placing a class of unique ineptitude, he had told Yale they ought not to take anyone at all. His views on Ricardo's chances at Harvard were not to be scorned. Kate, however, thought Leo's annoyance exaggerated.

"Who knows how Harvard decides anything?" she said. "Why concern yourself?"

So Leo did not discuss it any further. Kate wondered if she ought not to have truncated the conversation, her views on speaking to the young consisting almost entirely in the necessity to give them opportunities to communicate should they choose. She ought not to have put Leo down. The fact was, she was tired of the whole college business, and she realized, laying down her pen and giving herself over from work to consideration of Leo's school, sick to death of that institution.

For most of the year, attending basketball games and receiving from Leo what she only now began to realize were clear signals, she had failed, deliberately failed, to bring her distaste for St. Anthony's into focus. St. Anthony's was as different from the Theban, which Kate had attended and where she had lately taught a seminar, as—the proper simile eluded her, but seemed in the air—as the jet set from Back Bay.

The jet set, of course, was the point. The beautiful people. Money and media coverage. The wealth of Leo's friends, the lives they led, had already left Kate gasping. At the Theban, to spend money ostentatiously was as unacceptable as to admit to racial prejudice. One of Leo's friends had flown out to Indianapolis for the races; another had been given, in anticipation of graduation, a slick and expensive automobile. Was it the difference between boys' and girls' schools?

Kate thought not. St. Anthony's, after its period of high and quiet reputation, had, a decade ago, hired a headmaster whose job, as he clearly understood it, was to attract the right people with money, to swell the endowment fund, and build a new building adjoining the old. This he had done; St. Anthony's began attracting not only the children of prominent political figures and actors' children, but rich and generous new rich who would pay to have their children go to school with the children of the powerful and actors' children. But this headmaster, while good at social and financial matters, had never taught; his only skills were money and contacts, and his ego required that the men in administrative positions be inferior to himself. It was borne in upon Kate that one of the facts which made Leo and his friends insufferable was their knowledge that they were smarter, and with better values, than the men who ran the school.

"Well," Kate comforted herself, "I didn't choose the school, and in six weeks Leo will be through with it. What else, after all, can happen?" She wondered if Max knew the Ricardo boy. His view might be slightly more reasoned than Leo's. She added this point to her mental agenda for lunch with Max. Her thoughts returned, as they so often did, to Gerry Marston, who had died, now that she thought of it, on the rocks near the house of Ricardo's grandmother. An odd coincidence.

A further connection between what Kate thought of as the Max and the Leo questions was established on the day of Kate's luncheon with Max: she was to go from

70

the lunch at the Cosmopolitan Club to watch Leo pitch at a baseball game in Central Park. Reed had been scornful.

"I am put in mind," he said, "of Lord Randolph Churchill, who once, getting into the clutches of a bore at his club, rang the bell and said to the waiter, 'Would you mind listening to the end of this story?' and left the room."

"Meaning?" Kate had asked.

"Meaning if Leo needs an audience, ring for a middle-aged lady with nothing else to do, and ask her, 'Would you mind watching this game?' and get back to work."

"You might try coming yourself," Kate answered. "You like baseball better than basketball."

"Only marginally, as I would rather be shot than hanged. To think you would develop such an enthusiasm for manly sports."

"I despise football," Kate said.

"But if Leo had chosen to play it, you would have gone anyway, now wouldn't you?"

"Probably," Kate said. "Thank heaven for small favors. By the way, Ricardo plays shortstop."

"Who is Ricardo?"

"Remind me to tell you sometime," Kate said, departing for the Cos Club.

She and Max had a drink first in the comfortable lounge. Max settled down with the happy air he always assumed when surrounded by what he called civilization. The pleasant uniformed maid took their order. I expect I like the Cos Club, Kate thought to herself, because I am often one of the youngest people here, whereas I am one of the oldest people everywhere else.

"And how are you, Kate?" Max asked, guessing at her thoughts. "Not growing old and cranky like me?"

"I'm fine," Kate said, pulling herself together. "Except for a nagging curiosity about the Hutchins papers. What happened in the end, to the papers and the portrait and the house?"

"I take all those questions to mean that you really want an answer, and are prepared to have me hold forth at inordinate length, even for me. Cecily's remains, literary and other, have not been without adventures."

"You're not referring to her body, also?"

"Am I not? It turned out she wanted to be buried in the nearby cemetery in Maine, the town cemetery. She'd bought a plot, of course, when Ricardo died, so her body had to be brought back to be buried next to his. Her children, and the lawyer who is executor, and I all realized that fuss was the last thing Cecily wanted. She expected to die in her bed, and not in England, but, having died there, would no doubt have wanted to be buried with the rest of her family with the least possible derrydo. But—a will is a will, so back Cecily came, by plane to the Boston airport and thence by hearse to her burial place. We all rode along behind, but only days later, after the airport released the body. Customs officials, it transpires, are *very* suspicious of bodies. Anyway, Cecily is now safe in the earth. Her other remains were no less complicated. Are you certain you want to hear it all?"

"Utterly. Shall we go in to lunch? I've reserved a window table."

"Considerate as ever," Max said when they were seated. "Cecily once made a speech in the library here. Years ago. One of her rare public appearances, before she became all that famous. Remind me to tell you about it someday. Well, to make a long story short, as an exceedingly long-winded friend of mine used to say, I sold the papers to the Wallingford for a handsome sum; handsome. Her children thanked me, and with reason. You asked about the portrait. That crossed the ocean at more or less the same time as Cecily, going, of course, in the opposite direction. She left it to the Tate. It, too, would have brought a handsome price, no doubt, if auctioned at Sotheby's, but the lawyer saved her heirs from any unseemly regret by pointing out that the taxes on so large an estate as the one they inherited *plus* the portrait would have been downright confiscatory. As it was, I believe there was some tax diddling because of the gift, but I don't understand it and don't want to. One hires lawyers as one hires plumbers, because one wants to keep one's hands off the beastly drains. Plumbers, of course, are harder to find than lawyers, but we needn't go into that. Dorothy Whitmore is now in London, being viewed by hundreds every day, or so I am told. The house has been purchased for a stately sum, and the whole matter has resolved itself with perfect ease and graciousness, except that the children started interfering into my part of the business and stirring up trouble. They didn't understand Cecily, that's why she chose me as literary executor, a fact both the lawyer and I pointed out with some vigor and more than a little redundancy, but the trouble was the children came down on the side of some other library. Sheer greed, of course. Not on the part of the other library, which is above reproach; the children. Ah, I'm glad to see the roast pork is as good as ever."

"Go on," Kate said. "Don't stop just at the exciting part. I know it's rude of me to invite you to lunch and then not let you eat, but I must hear all."

"Which I am longing to tell, as you well know. You might respond from time to time, to allow me another mouthful. The problem, you see, was whether to cash in immediately on Cecily's growing reputation, greatly helped by what I resolutely refuse to call 'women's lib.' "

"I expected as much," Kate said. "All those women writers who've been ignored or forgotten for years are suddenly being rediscovered. I, for one, am glad. Apart from everything else, they provide new and exciting subjects for dissertations: one can have just so many studies of Tennyson's later imagery, and the closet dramas of Swinburne. And you feel Cecily would have wanted to be protected from peering eyes?"

"Not really, no. If she'd wanted her papers sealed, she would have said so. Of course, I would gladly have sealed them if it had been up to me, or burned them if it came to that—as we have discussed already. But as her literary executor, I had to abide by her wishes, which I interpreted as eventual publication and use of the papers, but not with unseemly haste or slipshod editorial work."

"Surely no library would allow slipshod editorial work."

"Naturally not. Nonetheless, with all sorts of people rushing in to get out editions, there is not only a danger but a likelihood of errors. Cecily would have wanted all that to await my biography and perhaps my edition of the letters."

"So you *are* doing a biography. Max, how exciting."

"Well, when you come right down to it, who is more qualified than I?"

"Do her children disagree?"

"Not as to my qualifications, no. At least, not to my face. But they want all of Cecily's books reissued with snappy introductions; they want anything that will increase the royalties. I point out that they will have the royalties in time, but they are afraid the demand for the work will pass. I accuse them of having little faith in their mother's work, and they accuse me of wanting to keep it all to myself. Needless to say, the whole matter is further complicated by the ambiguities inherent in the nebulous concept of the literary executor. But Cecily's will was clarity itself, and the papers have gone to the Wallingford. I have applied for leave from the university, and the Wallingford has offered me working space. Ah, I am pleased to see caramel custard."

"Naturally," Kate said, "I think of Gerry Marston. Suppose she had wanted to look at the papers for a study of Dorothy Whitmore. Wouldn't you have let her?"

"Eventually. But I would rather keep everything under control until the biography and a decent edition of the letters. Perhaps the manuscripts will be made available to qualified scholars, but not the papers generally. I know it sounds selfish and beastly, but believe me, my dear, it's the only way to handle these matters. Look at the James family. They gave Leon Edel complete domain until he finished the biography, and never regretted it. No doubt other scholars did, but what decision has ever made everyone happy?"

"It strikes me as odd," Kate said, looking around the Cosmopolitan Club. "Here we sit, in a women's club, discussing a woman writer whose work is certainly getting more attention because of the women's movement, and you have sold her papers to a stuffy male club that admits women only on occasional evenings and by special invitation."

"The exhibition hall and the library are open to women scholars, even if the lectures and the membership are not. My dear, they have to admit women to the building; they are a tax-free institution."

Max sat back a moment. "I am not, you know, as insensitive as you think. Cecily did know me, and did choose me because she wanted not only discretion but, if you will forgive the expression, guts. The simple ability to say no and stick by it, particularly in the face of the outraged young, seems to be a lost or vestigial skill. Cecily counted on my hard heart and stern demeanor. Which is not to say I shall never, if, for example, a personal request is made by you, allow some use of the papers. But it is best to begin with a reputation for intransigence. You are also, how could you not be, thinking of that unfortunate child killed on the rocks. You cannot quite rid your mind, can you, Kate, of the horrible thought that I might somehow have willed her death in order not to have to show her the papers, if any, which allude to Dorothy Whitmore. She has doubtless risen in your mind as a martyr to scholarship, just the sort I am doing my best to discourage. But I would like gently to remind you that my passion for civilization and culture in the truest sense makes me loathe

76

any sort of violent solution to a problem. What you suspect me of I cannot imagine, but ought we not to get your grisly thoughts out in the open?"

"I'm sorry, Max. I've been harboring not suspicions, of course, but certain feelings of uneasiness. Somehow your attitude toward the papers is inextricably connected in my mind with her death."

"That's not surprising. It would be surprising if they weren't connected. But do let me point out, my adorably feminine and therefore basically irrational creature, however brilliant, that she didn't know I was literary executor or had the smallest connection with the papers. There was no connection between us. While she was up there, whatever she was doing, I was being my particularly busy self at your university and mine."

"You shame me, Max. But I'm glad it's out in the open. It wasn't really suspicion, you must see that. Just uneasiness. By the way, were Cecily's children in England the week Gerry died?"

"Yes, they were, if you insist on seeking out all possible suspects. Dear Kate, I hope you haven't picked more tiring investigative habits from your husband. My hope was that he would *not* encourage you in these matters. The children stayed on with Cecily to visit old friends."

"We keep referring to the childen; they must be as old as I."

"They are, my dear; no allowances for gallantry. Hold on and let me get the dates clear in my head."

"Shall we have coffee in the lounge?"

"An excellent suggestion." In was obvious that as they rose from the table Max, as he pulled out her chair, was doing figures in his head. "I may have been too gallant," he said, when Kate had ordered coffee, "but I don't know when you were born and don't intend to ask. Cecily's children were born in the early thirties. Roger is the oldest, then Thad, then Claudia. They all have children, but perhaps you'll spare me the arithmetic of that."

"As a matter of fact," Kate said, "no. I've just met one of those children. A boy in my nephew's class at St. Anthony's, about to graduate and go to Harvard."

"Is he indeed? Well, Harvard had better standards in former years. Still, the young do change, and it's a while since I saw him. He's Roger's son. I can't say I've ever cared for Roger. He married a wealthy woman from some banking house, and went to work for them. Apparently his response to an artistic household was to become as bourgeois as possible; not hard to understand, I dare say. He's overindulged his children, who strut a bit too much, as does he."

"I'm off now to see him play baseball in Central Park. Would you care to come?"

"Kate, I fear for your immortal soul, not to mention your sanity."

"I know, but Leo likes me to come, heaven knows why. Why are you so surprised that Roger's son got into Harvard?"

"I thought they had better taste, put simply. It's not as though he's one of those with double seven hundreds in the College Boards, or any talent. Nor that good an athlete, I should think. Can he be their token wasp?"

"From all I've heard, Harvard is as male and as wasp as ever; it can't be that. Who was the nephew whose wedding Cecily and children attended, and you didn't."

"Ah. That's personal history and more easily and accurately explained. My mother and Cecily were always close friends, as I told you. Ever since Oxford. Naturally they kept in touch with each other, as did their children in time. My sister, Muriel, married an Englishman, who is, in fact, master of a college at Cambridge. It was her son whose nuptials called from afar."

"And you, the only living uncle, didn't appear."

"I'm not the only living uncle. I have a brother named Herbert, who, like me, came to America and is an academician, in science, however, but who happens to be spending part of this year in Oxford. So the nephew was not uncleless at all."

"Max, forgive me my feverish and unclear thoughts."

"There is nothing to forgive, my dear. What's more, I invite you at any time to come and look at anything you like at the Wallingford. Can I say handsomer than that? I shall tell the librarian, a delightful young man by the name of Sparrow, that under no circumstances are you to be eschewed for your sex or for any other reason. Perhaps a glance through the papers and a count of the boxes of papers will calm the most feverish imaginings."

"Good," Kate said. "I shall take you and the Wallingford up on your offer. But there is one other question nagging at me, Max. Why did you feel trepidations about going up to Maine by yourself when the prowler had been seen or whatever it was?"

"Ghosts, my dear. I have never disbelieved in ghosts, only in their more dramatic physical manifestations. Somehow I did not want to go back to that house alone, without someone to exchange impressions with; I

79

wanted to talk about Cecily, preparing myself for the appraiser. He duly came, which I neglected to tell you, and was notably impressed. His appraisal took three days and exceeded all our expectations. But that first day, even the most confirmed bachelor, as the cliché has it, perhaps especially he, wants to have his hand held occasionally. Usually there are women hovering about, simply aching to help. I went in search of you across fields of hay because I thought you would be the one to talk to about Cecily. Very vague, I'm afraid, and unreassuring. If it hadn't been for the coincidence of that beastly girl—well, forgive me, my dear, but I didn't know her and can scarcely applaud her demise upon Cecily's rocky coast—I think our whole trip would have been a human and enlightening experience."

"Well," Kate said, "if I had a glass, I would raise it in a toast to you and the biography."

six

Later, seated in Central Park in the blazing sun, Kate wished for a glass from thirst, rather than the desire to toast anything. True, a pushwagon was dispensing to the young Coca-Cola or an imitation thereof, but Kate had long since decided that while three weeks spent, waterless, on the desert might render Coca-Cola attractive, she doubted it. St. Anthony's was playing against a Catholic prep school; it was clear that baseball was not their game. St. Anthony's, on the other hand, played with what seemed to Kate sinister competence. That one was supposed to slide into base with one's spikes aimed at the baseman Kate had already heard, to her horror. That one could jeer at the pitcher to upset him and run into players for no other reason than to do them injury, appalled her further. She said as much to Leo as he joined her on the outside bench, when his team was up at bat and Leo had been replaced, since St. Anthony's was so far ahead.

"Oh, what the hell," Leo said. "That's the game. In spring training, the Texas Rangers were throwing bean balls at the Yankees, and there was a real rumble."

"Bean balls?"

"Really, Kate, don't you ever read the paper? The

pitcher was throwing them at the batter, trying to injure their best men. Billy Martin's idea."

"You can't be serious."

"Naturally the other team doesn't like that."

"Naturally. Or I guess naturally. Leo, whatever happened to the old idea about, it doesn't matter if you win or lose, it's how you play the game."

"Victorian, I suppose."

"Yes, silly of me. As Joseph Kennedy said to his sons, get in there and win. As Vince Lombardi said to Nixon or somebody, winning isn't important, it's just everything. The connection with Watergate shall go unremarked upon. Are you sure you want to sit here with an aging aunt? Is anything wrong, Leo?"

"Some schools at basketball games hold back the clock on the home court. We never do that."

"Obviously you're all in line for the Nobel Prize. I always promised myself when young that I would never say, when old, what is the world coming to? Please notice that I haven't said it. Leo, is everything quite all right? You don't usually sit with me, do you? You usually sit on the bench." This was a fine distinction, since the "bench" within the playing field and the one just outside the fence on which Kate sat were indistinguishable.

"Really, Kate, you don't have to go on acting as though no male ever talked to an older woman. Some of my friends said they'd like to meet you when they heard you were a professor. Of course, they'd rather meet Reed and hear about the district attorney's office."

"Have you suggested such a meeting to him?"

"It just has to happen. Well, see you."

Kate watched him drop back onto the bench where

82

sat the team. What could be wrong? she asked herself. He's just chosen Swarthmore over Harvard, scarcely a cause for depression. I must be getting fanciful, the price, no doubt, of associating with the young. At this point the coach yelled: "O.K., Ricardo, out. Back to the showers."

This last, in the wilds of Central Park, she took to be a humorous remark. "Good game," the coach said. "Yeah, man," was echoed from the team. Kate watched Ricardo as he strolled (strutted, lurched, shambled) back to the bench. She tried to see, somewhere, in his countenance, a painter from Europe, a woman writer of infinite sensibility. She saw him sit next to Leo, and Leo greeted him, but, after a moment, Leo moved away. A movement, Kate sternly told herself, without significance. Leo seemed in search of a bat. Catching his eye Kate waved goodbye and strolled homeward across the park.

Once home, she turned to her accumulated correspondence—accumulated in the sense that dust accumulates under a bed. Lunch and baseball must be paid for by hours with the typewriter. It seemed improbable that a mere professor of literature (as opposed, for example, to a famous author like Cecily) could receive so much mail. Reed, in his practical way, had suggested ignoring it, hiring a secretary, using a dictaphone. Kate found none of these satisfactory. She did not even make use of the secretaries in the office, but typed out her own letters and hoped that by the end of a long evening's work syntax, spelling, and sanity had been maintained.

The National Endowment for the Humanities, youth grant division, wondered if she would serve as a consultant, and had suggested to the young man in question that he write her. He began his letter: "Kate," and concluded it: "Your friend Andy," though she had, of course, never heard of him until this moment. She tried hard not to let what was, after all, merely another and probably no less noble code of behavior influence her response to his proposal. Reading it, she discovered she was not the proper person to serve as consultant, but thought she knew who was. This involved a letter to that person, one to the young man, one to the NEH, and a generous distribution of carbons all around.

There were eleven requests for recommendations from students and former students; these Kate guiltily put aside, swearing to herself that she would get up half an hour early and do them when she was fresh, in every sense of the word. Publishers wanted her opinion about books ("We will, of course, pay a small honorarium"). Announcements of meetings on every conceivable subject (either she was more in demand, or deans were more numerous and given to busy work, almost certainly the latter) did not require a written response. She tore up several publishers' announcements of freshman English handbooks (there is some advantage in growing long in the tooth, let it not be forgotten) and put aside for future perusal publishers' catalogues of forthcoming books. This brought her to a letter from England. Now, who on earth, Kate wondered, but not for long. "Dear Kate," the letter began, "this is from me, Phyllis, your friend that was. I am no more because there is no place for women at Oxford, be they neither students nor dons. To think that I complained about overwork. If I ever do so again, you have my permission to slap me sharply in the face, three times. Hugh is madly happy, of course, and no one at Oxford worries about wives. They are expected to have a good tea ready, to keep the children in hand, and to see to the laundry. What a life, even without children.

"Which is to say please, if there remains any charity in your soul, come for a couple of weeks after classes and visit Oxford and talk to me; I yearn for conversation with a sane human being, especially one with views on America—you know, Nixon, the oil crisis, and the Equal Rights Amendment. I'll gladly pay your fare if you are no longer rich and can't afford it. Also, I'll put you up here, but, candidly, I don't advise it. When you arrive (you see I say 'when,' not 'if'; I'm already counting on it) and see the place, you'll understand my apparent lack of hospitality. I'll reserve you a room at the best local hotel, the moment I hear that you will come, and when. Were you male, one could get you an invitation somewhere, even All Souls, who knows, but being female, you will have to pig it in a hotel. Write yes by return mail. That will give me hope for the next weeks, and a reason to go on living. I can't just leave Hugh and go home, or travel, because that will prove to all the world that I am nothing but a compulsive idiot and unable to spend a year with my husband like a proper wife, as everyone has long suspected. And they're right, damn it."

Reed appeared in the doorway, recalling Kate from a daydream of Oxford and long thoughts of rediscovering Cecily Hutchins, and Dorothy Whitmore, or at the least, chasing their ghosts through what remained of the Oxford of their youth.

"Drink? Or are you on the verge of a peroration and not to be jostled?"

"I'd love a drink, and some conversation. I hope your day was all right, because I don't mean to ask you about it; I want to tell you about mine."

"Bound to be more interesting than mine, even if you only watched Leo play baseball. I take it there is more than that."

"Much more," Kate said, as they settled down in the living room and Reed brought in the tray with the makings of drinks. "First of all, I've had a letter. From Phyllis, who is going mad from boredom and the female life in Oxford generally. She'd like me to visit her when my term is over, in May. Any objections?"

"I knew Phyllis's taking a year off like that was madness. We both told her repeatedly, if I remember, and with rising emphasis, that she should *not* immure herself in Oxford because she would simply cease to exist as a person. It appears that she has."

"And yet, you know," Kate said, accepting a martini, "I think I understand Phyllis very well. It's why, if you've no violent objections, I'll join her for a week or two. Quite apart from wanting a change of pace and a vacation from her job, and all that, she'd been as besotted with the idea of Oxford all her life as I have been. Somehow one always assumes that at Oxford one will end up mysteriously dining in hall with someone from a Michael Innes novel. But of course, it isn't like that at all. Yet you know, if someone were to ask me to come dine at the high table even today, I'd go like a shot—all the way across the Atlantic. Phyllis probably felt the same. She couldn't really believe that she'd end up never meeting anyone at Oxford except as Hugh's wife, and not often then. Oxford dons treat their wives the way most Americans treat their lovers, as a sort of

86

shameful necessity. Still, if, knowing all that, I had one wish right now, it would be to be connected for a time with an Oxford college and dine at the high table, chat in the SCR, and have port in the combination room."

"You are an incurable romantic," Reed said, "and you loathe port. But I see nothing wrong with acting out one's dreams, if only to discover that they never had a shred of reality about them. But I trust, Kate, I do most earnestly trust, that you are not going off to Oxford on some mad chase after that author your student was working on. Oh, my God, I see that you are. You shall doubtless find that she spent her entire Oxford career writing inferior poetry, attending mixed parties, and making speeches, and was sent down with a poor third after flirting with the dons on the *viva voce*."

"Well"—Kate looked sheepish—"I would never have thought of it on my own bat. But it did occur to me that if I were to go there to help Phyllis face the facts about England, I might just case the joint—meaning Somerville College, where Cecily Hutchins and Dorothy Whitmore and Max's mother came up for their last Trinity term over half a century ago. You know, Reed, they bicycled on Broad Street, under the gaze of the twelve Caesars, and fed the carp in the pool at Christ Church, and sat beneath the great copper beech in the Wadham garden. And somehow I long to follow in their footsteps."

"Oh, Lord," Reed said, "and after only one martini. A bad, bad case. Can it be that cases of Anglophilia, like poison ivy, get worse each time?"

What Kate might have answered was never to be known; into the living room at that moment walked Leo. He immediately collapsed, as was his wont, onto a wing chair, which he nonetheless sprawled in as though it were a chaise longue. The effect, of a figure in pain posing for Michelangelo, was in no way diminished by Leo's expression. It was not usual for Leo to appear at this hour, or in this way. His time before meals (when he attended meals) was devoted to sleeping, or telephoning, or drinking Coke and consuming calories in their sweetest and most lethal form. If he drank alcohol, it was not before meals, and not with Kate and Reed.

Vigorously, Kate restrained herself from asking if anything was the matter. Leo's appearance indicated a need to talk, and a direct question would be death to that necessity. There was a long silence, broken only by Reed's ice cubes bumping in the cocktail shaker.

"Wouldn't it be illegal to try and bug someone in a locker room?" Leo at last asked.

Reed's spilling a good portion of one martini indicated he was as startled by the question as was Kate. "Illegal? Of course it's illegal. At the same time, as is said about everything else these days, from bribery to assassination, everybody does it. As evidence in court, it's worthless."

"What do you mean, everybody does it?" Kate asked.

"There are times," Reed said, "when I long to call you Goody Two-Shoes. Every businessman has a dictaphone with a plug all ready for his phone. He's not supposed to use it without telling the other chap, but he just wants a record for his files, so he tells himself. It's not unusual, as I understand it, to bug the company plane, and then send the chaps who are dealing with you on a merger home in it. What better way to find out what deal they're ready to settle for? Or you bug

88

the men's room. These days the women's room, too, I guess. You have heard of Watergate?"

"But everyone in the White House knew."

"Everyone who was planning hanky-panky in the Oval Office; but what about the chaps on the other end of the line; of the visiting heads of state, if it comes to that? Probably they're used to it."

"Can't you go to jail for it?" Leo asked. "That's what I told them."

"Leo," Reed said, "I have a horrible feeling that we should stop discussing bugging locker rooms and all the legal aspects thereof, and get down to cases. Are you planning to bug a locker room?"

"I'm against it," Leo said.

"How on earth would you do it?" Kate asked.

"Really, Kate, I hardly think that's the point at the moment."

"You sound just like a father in the movies," Kate said. "Honestly, Leo, I'm horrified, of course, but madly curious."

"A lot of the guys go in for electronics; there's all kinds of surveillance apparatus. The Pentagon owns loads."

"The question is not why you chose Swarthmore over Harvard, but how you got into either place, with all that clarity of mind and language. Never mind, you can explain it to me another time, when we're making conversation, waiting for you to come up to bat."

"Harvard and Swarthmore is the whole point. Harvard anyhow. Oh, shit."

Looking at Leo, Kate realized that had he been ten years younger, or even eight, he would have begun to cry. That being unthought of in our culture, he was

89

banging his fists, one into the other, and against his thighs. His body rocked back and forth in the chair, for whose legs and webbing Kate decided to abandon all consideration. Her mother, she thought with a certain satisfaction, would have worried about the chair above all else.

"Leo," Reed said, "is there a beginning to this story, or are you still collecting stray information and trying to get it to hang together? You know, you can tell us, and then forget you did. Or you can ask questions, and take them away in the corner and chew on them. But if you want to discuss this at all, and I rather get the impression that you do, could we try to get the points into some sort of order, rational, logical, or sequential, as you prefer?"

For the first time Leo smiled. "Reed, you're getting to talk like Kate. Does that always happen to married people?"

"Alas, no," Reed said. "Kate simply talks more like Kate, and not a bit like me."

"Well," Leo said, "you know all about College Boards?"

Reed and Kate stared at him. As rhetorical questions go, this could have stood as the model for them all. Perhaps there exist, somewhere, parental figures of a college-bound (as the jargon has it) adolescent who do *not* know about the College Boards, but one would have to guess that their relation with their progeny was offhand to the point of downright neglect. College Boards serve the college admissions officers as scholarship examinations serve whatever they call admissions at Oxford and Cambridge. You may get in on money and athletics, or a combination of both, but high scores on the College Boards are the surest way. No college will admit this, of course, but it is so nonetheless. Any student who is in the middle seven hundreds on both math and verbal tests—eight hundred being perfect—is in for serious consideration from any college admissions board anywhere. Many other factors are taken into account; where students with lower scores must be chosen, other factors loom large. If, however, a student has goodish recommendations, goodish grades, or a certain amount of discernible talent, but Board scores only in the five hundreds, his chances for the big colleges are not great.

Kate had her own views on these tests, and she was, moreover, willing to expound them, asked or not. In her opinion, they were the lazy way out. Take medical schools, for instance, who had exams (now called Medical Boards) administered by the very same people, and Kate thought the results disastrous. Whatever medical schools said, they tended to take the student with A's in organic chemistry and high Board scores, which went partway—Kate thought a very long way indeed—toward explaining the sort of doctors and medical care with which the country was saddled. But that was neither here nor there, and Kate tried to divert her mind from this byway.

"Yes," Reed said, watching Kate's face as her thoughts rapidly covered the familiar territory. "We know about College Boards. What comes next?"

"I didn't take any SAT's this November, but some other guys—"

"What did you take?"

"I took achievement tests, at another time, in special subjects; that's altogether different." Leo's voice had immediately attained that tone reserved for adolescents explaining something not for the first time to parents, or adults they could treat as parents. That they themselves frequently required explanations many times repeated never, of course, occurred to them. Adolescence was not the time for such thoughts: one cannot be thoughtful and have an identity crisis simultaneously, which, Kate thought, is the best reason for learning manners when young I've ever heard. She dragged back her wandering thoughts. "Yes," she said, "I remember now: you didn't take the SAT's over because you'd done so well on them the first time."

"Well, frankly, I figured, why push your luck?"

"A wise decision, I'm sure. Who did take them over? I mean," she hastened to add before sounding dim-witted and being immediately reprimanded, "whose luck needed pushing?"

"Ten guys. Their names don't matter at this point," Leo said darkly. "Except that one of them was Ricardo."

"Ah, and one gathers he did rather better the second time around." Reed began, it was clear to Kate, to hope that he was dealing with a simple case of juvenile resentment.

"A lot better." Leo's voice was so full of sarcasm his lip began to curl, an effect Kate could not remember having noticed before. "He got 760 on the verbal, and 420 on the math."

"Well, 420 wouldn't get him into Harvard would it?" Kate had the feeling she often got when Leo explained why a catcher couldn't be left-handed. Not so Reed.

"In other words," Reed said, "someone took the test

for him, but he was too smart to try to get a high score on the math."

"Exactly. Of course, when you can get a perfect score yourself on the math, it's a little hard to know how many mistakes to make on purpose, and ... the guy who took them, he mucked it up a bit. But the 760 on the verbal got him, the first guy, into Harvard, along with all his other so-called qualifications. I think it shits."

"Leo," Kate said, putting down her drink and feeling, suddenly, cold sober. "Surely there's some surveillance, surely someone—"

"Surely, crap." Kate decided, under the circumstances, to ignore Leo's language, which always increased in obscenity in proportion to his emotion.

"How was it done, then?"

"Look, there's a room full of guys taking the test, from schools all over the city. You sign your name and fill out a form. So the guy, the first guy, learns to write like the second guy; who's to know? That's only one way of cheating. The commoner way is on the achievement tests; you say you want to take four: history, math, French, chemistry. Then you spend all four hours on one, cancel the scores on the others, which you're allowed to do, and have had four hours on a test that other people only get one on. I know a guy who did that, and someone found out, and the College Board people did nothing. They can't afford to. They've got a monopoly, and they don't want to make waves."

"Leo," Kate said. "May we ignore ways of cheating on the achievement tests for a moment, though I shall return to that at a later time and become hysterical? For the moment we are with the SAT's. You are telling us

93

that one boy can take the test for another, and there is no way this can be prevented. These tests are not policed at all?"

"Nope. Of course, the first guy forged the second guy's name and went as him."

"Wasn't Harvard suspicious of this sudden rise in the score of the boy we may perhaps call Ricardo?"

"Not really; they do actually happen sometimes. Also, by this time Ricardo had started to play up his writing grandmother, and he's a pretty smooth guy—he sounded like maybe he was going to write great novels, and he *is* good in English, and the teachers in English who like him don't know he's a shit, and they've all heard of his grandmother. Once Harvard had that new SAT score, well, O.K."

"Is it possible," Reed said, "that in my own living room I am discovering why so many fools and knaves are lawyers? Can you get someone to take the Law Boards for you?"

"Relax, Reed," Leo said. "I wondered about that, too. They fingerprint you there. No way."

"Do you know something?" Kate said. "Leo can sneer if he wants to, but I can't imagine such a thing happening at the Theban."

To her surprise, Leo, who sometimes grew tired of hearing the virtues of the Theban expounded, agreed with her. "That's exactly what's getting to us. Some of us," he added darkly. "The whole school's been a PR trip from the beginning—success was all that mattered, smoothness, grades, being cool. Naturally this happened."

"It occurs to me to wonder—well, many things,"

Reed said. "To start with the least important, who is, or was, Ricardo's grandmother?"

"Cecily Hutchins," Kate said.

"My God. I might have guessed, I suppose. Who else could it possibly have been, given the Fansler family?"

"I'm sure I don't know what you mean by that remark," Kate said.

"Neither do I," Reed agreed. "Leo, I get the picture, more or less, leaving out for a moment the start of this conversation, which had to do with electronic surveillance in locker rooms. I trust we shall return to that, as MacArthur to the Philippines. What is it, in the midst of all this, that's bugging you, if you'll forgive the expression. That someone cheated, that the system doesn't work, that boys you like better didn't get into the college they wanted because they were honest—where's it at?"

"If you are going to sound like a superannuated rock star, I refuse to continue the conversation," Kate said, "or let you continue it. Obscenity I shall agree to ignore, but certain argots are forbidden. Absolutely."

"Oh, Jesus," Leo said. "It just shits."

"Is there something you think you should do about it?" Reed asked.

"I know you think I shouldn't," Leo said. "Everyone thinks no one should. One of them said it's a code in all the prep schools. But it's not just that Finlay lied to me."

"Finlay?"

"The guy who took the test; he's a genius."

"If he's such a genius, couldn't he have figured this out as being goddamned stupid?" There was no question about it, Reed was upset. Kate thought she was beginning to guess why.

"I shouldn't have told you the names."

"We've settled that already. The relief is enormous; I was beginning to get those two guys who did this and that as confused as two ballplayers. How did Finlay lie to you?"

"Ricardo told me Finlay'd taken the test for him. He bragged about it. I asked Finlay, and Finlay said he hadn't. He lied."

"Funny thing, but according to Jimmy Breslin, that's why the good guys won over Watergate. They minded being lied to," Kate observed.

Leo, though an admirer of Jimmy Breslin, ignored this.

"Of course," he said, "most of the guys say you don't interfere. But Ricardo and Finlay interfered themselves, didn't they? Guys I like didn't get into Harvard. And then they've been bragging about it. But the real fucker is, the school knows and isn't doing a damn thing." Leo leaned back with some relief; he had brought out the main point.

"How do you know the school knows?"

" 'Cause someone told the headmaster. I know that." It was clear there were ranges of confidences Leo was not prepared to scale. "So he called in Finlay and Ricardo, and they told him it wasn't true. But he knows it's true. Only he's scared Finlay's father, who owns Wyoming or something, will sue the hell out of them. And he'd rather not rock the boat. This sort of mess is not good for the school's image."

"But the fact that the whole senior class knows this,

and that the Watergate code is being adhered to, doesn't worry him, is that it?" Kate asked.

"Could we stop talking about Watergate," Reed said. "I know, you're right; this is what Watergate is all about. I withdraw the request. Leo, you know, I assume, what damn near every parent in America would say to you now if you came to them with this story; they'd say it was awful, but they'd advise you as their child not to get involved. Because in the end, you always get it in the neck. Righteousness is a very unpopular stand. We like people to do our dirty work for us, but we reserve the right to call them moralistic bastards when they do. That's why it was only Nixon's insane folly that forced politicians against him. I know, I know, we're not discussing Watergate."

"I don't know what to do anyway," Leo said, grumbling. "I'm just pissed, like lots of others. Well, some others."

Reed looked at him. "Something has occurred to you. What?

"It's not my idea, really. It's a few of the other guys. They said we ought at least to mention it to the faculty. Give them a chance to know. And talk about it a little, around. Just don't let it die. Finlay and Ricardo will probably kill us," he added. "That, or they'll plant heroin on me and call the cops."

Reed and Kate stared at him. He would be eighteen in a few months. Part of him was adult, already knowing the risk, estimating the cost, deciding what the truth and the law were worth. Another part of him was a child, scared, as he would have said, shitless.

Kate spoke first. "The biggest mistake would be to be arrogant about it, or righteous, or anything like that."

Reed said, "I take it most of the others want to let it alone."

"Yeah. They say you can't interfere in someone's life. But when does that stop? I mean we all cheat, I admit that, but you gotta draw the line."

"Why in hell can't they police those tests properly?" Kate asked.

"Might we return to this bugging idea a minute, Leo?" Reed asked. "Does that fit in here somewhere?"

"I could go to jail," he said darkly.

"You and the other boys with the electronics. Meanwhile, what were you after?"

"Those two, they're such smooth liars. They brag about what they do, but they can deny it so convincingly. Finlay lied to me, one of his closest friends."

"Not to mention the headmaster."

"Yeah. So . . ."

"So you wanted it recorded. I take it the point was to get them to brag about it in the locker room. An excellent place for bragging, I'll give you that."

"That's what the others think, Reed," Leo said. "Their idea was, even if we couldn't tell about the bugging, at least we'd *know*. I'm against it; we know anyway. That's not the point. It's whether to do anything about it at school."

"Can you remember"—Reed turned to Kate—"the last time we had three martinis?"

"I can; the circumstances are in no way appropriate to this occasion."

"So you mean," Leo said, "that unlike all those other parents, you think I ought to do what I want to do, if I want to do it?"

Reed mixed the drinks before answering. "I will

never be a parent, Leo, except in so far as I have been one to you, and I haven't a right in the world to propound the duties of parenthood. Nonetheless, I will. Parents are either (in the minds of their children) the voice for law and reason and covenants kept, or they are nothing. Acting as a parent, I shall therefore be such a voice. But don't expect glory. Most people who fight for law start out with the idea that they're going to be thanked. All they are is spit at. You can only fight for law because you think it so important you're unable to do anything else. Would anybody like to hire me as a commencement speaker? My fees are low, and my style rambling."

"I wonder what Cecily Hutchins would have thought of all this," Kate said. But what she really wondered was what Gerry Marston would have thought of it all. Or, if it came to that, Max.

Later that evening, after a dinner devoted to the rehashing of the whole St. Anthony's business—for only after people have asked questions, and explored many approaches, have they begun to reach the point of decision—and after Leo had retired, Reed's thoughts also turned to Max.

"Did you learn anything earth-shaking, or at least consoling, in your lunch today? You never had a chance to tell me, after all."

"I'm as easy as Max can make me, and inclined to attribute other feelings to my overheated imagination, a diagnosis with which I know you agree, on principle if not otherwise. I still don't know what that girl was doing there, excepting being brave and adventuresome. But why go out on the rocks? Still, I answer myself,

I—I, a middle-aged and supposedly sensible person—went out on the rocks. So there I am, in circles, dear Reed, as is my wont. Would you care to join the dance?"

"England will be a rest for you. When does your term end?"

"The first week in May, if I'm very wicked and dash off at the end of classes without waiting to be hauled onto some committee or examination or other. But do you think I ought to go? And leave Leo in the midst of all this, I mean?"

"Kate, really. You're coming all over female guilt. You're not his mother, and in any case, what can you do? By early May the whole matter will be in a different phase, if not utterly transformed. Maternal women are always sacrificing themselves to their children, only to find their children have no need of them at that point. In any case, Leo is almost eighteen."

"Reed, you are a perceptive man, though I forget to mention it as a rule. I've noticed just what you mean. Female guilt. A woman professor I know, very important, too, canceled all her courses for the rest of the semester because her husband had a heart attack. Well, it was damn worrying, and I sympathized. But one little part of me kept asking: would he have canceled his courses if she had had a heart attack? And the answer, of course, was no; he would have worried, and used old notes, and spent all the time he could with her, but he would have figured out that canceling his classes didn't accomplish a thing. But the woman professor was worried about how heartless she would look if she went about business as usual. Quite unwomanly."

"Exactly. Go to England. And do remember, you

can be back within ten hours, if need be. Would you hesitate about going to St. Louis?"

"Indefinitely. Why would anyone want to go to St. Louis?"

"Ah. You sound more like yourself. Tell me about Max." And when Kate had told him, he said there was no better place for anyone's papers than the Wallingford, if it was somewhat backward in its manners, and why didn't Kate call up the chap in charge of Cecily's papers and chat about one thing and another?

seven

Mr. Sparrow, librarian of the Wallingford, turned out, when Kate had lunch with him two days later, to be elegant, which was expected, and young, which was not; to have wit and manners, which was expected, and rather liberal ideas, which was not; in short, a phenomenon, all things considered, and a pleasant surprise.

"You have no idea," he said to Kate, whose invitation to luncheon he had accepted with a graciousness sufficiently bordering upon eagerness to be flattering but not daunting, "what an admirer I have been all these years of Cecily Hutchins. I was so desperately hoping we could meet the other library's offer, I can't tell you. Not that it ever came down to anything as crass as bidding for the papers—such does not happen in the more rarefied regions of New York's bibliographic world. But the heirs wanted money, and Mr. Reston wanted us, and it was clear that if we could find the money it would be us. I dream, needless to say, of an unpublished novel, which, it's pretty certain, we won't find. What I think I have found, and will soon show you, is an autobiographical fragment. Delicious. It's sketchy and yet it marvelously reverberates. I think it will have to be one of the first items published. Even Mr. Reston's agreed to that."

"Hasn't he asked you to call him Max?"

"No, he hasn't, and quite properly, too. Name-dropping and first-name-calling on short acquaintance are equally frowned upon at Wallingford, I'm glad to say. I detest being called Anthony, or worse, Tony, by people I scarcely know, particularly since no one who knows me ever calls me either. I'm called Tate, because of a youthful fascination with that museum when the family visited London one summer."

"That settles it; we will definitely stick to the formal address. The Kate, Tate exchange sounds too much like a first reader for comfort."

"My mind rather ran to limericks."

"Yet I do think of her as Cecily," Kate said, "and she old, famous, and dead."

"So do I. One must, when one's thought of a person intimately for over twenty years. I first read her when I was eleven. It was the novel about a family who go to spend the summer in France with friends. All girls, except for one eleven-year-old boy, who was, of course, me. But before I was through I was all of them. The great thing about Cecily was that the last novel was the best—not that usual, when one is seventy-three. No wonder her reputation picked up."

"Helped a bit by the new interest in women writers."

"Well, we could scarcely go on in America worshiping forever manly types on the hunt for animal flesh. Have pity."

"I had a student," Kate said, referring no more closely to the dead girl, "who had developed an interest in that generation at Oxford, particularly at Somerville. What I had hoped Max would allow was a search through Cecily's papers for some account of those years. Put together with the others we have, by Vera Brittain and so forth, it would make a fascinating study. Don't you agree?"

"I do, but I'm not sure Mr. Reston does. No doubt he's shying off because his mother was one of that Oxford generation. Or perhaps he thinks the emphasis should be on her fiction; I'm inclined to agree there."

"Well," Kate said, "as director of dissertations, I must be allowed a certain crass, businesslike interest in literary history. An account of that war generation of women at Oxford would certainly be more welcome than another analysis of the society of *Middlemarch*. Do you know anything about Dorothy Whitmore?"

"Funny you should ask that. I read about her picture going to the Tate, and I called the people over at the Gotham Book Mart to see if they had any of her books. They said that every now and then they sell the only one of her books they can get, *North Country Wind*, the popular one that was published after her death and was made into a movie."

"Mr. Sparrow, what if I were to follow you back to your lair right now? Might I have a peek?"

"I'd be pleased and honored. Professor Fansler, all considerations of graduate students and Oxford generations aside, Reston will do a stunning biography. He's one of those scholars and writers—how shall I put this delicately and with decorum—who sound opinionated in conversation, but who become translucent to the ideas and life of the subject whose life he is writing. If it's the right subject—and I think Cecily is; I think he is really attracted to her and her life—with his English upbringing and American experience, he'll be able to understand her more than we could. Do you know why she came to America?"

"Ricardo came to America, and where Ricardo went, Cecily went. Do you know anything about Ricardo?" Kate asked, as she followed Sparrow into the street.

"A little. He was a painter, and hired over here by the museums and rich collectors, rather like Roger Fry except that he lasted. They didn't retire to the Maine coast until later years, when he resumed painting. He was considerably older than Cecily and died first, though he lived to a grand old age. Cecily, I suppose, could write anywhere; certainly they revisited England often enough. What is odd is that none of their children is the least artistic; I don't believe the daughter even does watercolors."

"Perhaps that's why Cecily felt close to Max. It's odd about parents and children, I've often noticed. Particularly when both parents are dynamic beings and richly gifted, the children seem to aspire to ordinariness. Or anyway to achieve it."

They had by this time reached the front door of the Wallingford, a building donated to the organization that bore his name by its builder and owner. It had been designated a landmark, inside and out. "Which means," Sparrow said, after greeting a white-haired black man at the door who looked as though he had been sent from Central Casting for a Southern film in the late thirties and hadn't aged a minute since, "that we can't change a thing, not so much as the color of the paint, without a by-your-leave. A damnable nuisance, and expensive in one way, but at least it protects us from any wild schemer who might seize power at the Wallingford, not," he added, bowing Kate from the elevator on the third and library floor, "that that's very likely. It's a mixed blessing, in short, like most things, being a landmark, but we rather expect to make a trifle more on the swings than we lose on the roundabouts. The boxes wait, exciting and unpacked, in here."

The library at the Wallingford, modeled after the Duke of Humphrey's room in the Bodleian, looked marvelously inviting. But they passed through it without so much as a glance, to a small room beyond. Here, neatly piled, were an amazing number of cardboard boxes. "All well ordered, too," Sparrow said. "Correspondence, more or less alphabetical, manuscripts, and working journals. All going back to early days; apparently when she came to America she brought all the early stuff with her, heaven knows why. Still, we're glad she did. The appraiser, between ourselves, was beside himself with admiration."

"If this is all so organized," Kate said, "the letters to and from Dorothy Whitmore ought to be in the last box. I assume she didn't have scads of correspondents clustered at the end of the alphabet, their names beginning with y or z."

"All this harping on Whitmore; what can it be in aid of? And here I thought you were panting to see my autobiographical fragment."

"I am," Kate said. "Panting. In fact, I want to sit down, pretend I'm at the Bodleian, and read right through it now, if you'll allow me. Might I glance at the letters to you-know-who?"

"The answer is actually no. Since it's you, I'll give you a peek, so you can see how organized everyone has been—from Cecily, through dear careful Max, the appraiser, the packers, and, of course, wonderful us. Here are the Whitmore letters—there are not that many of them—but then they were together much of their youth and didn't write."

"What about after Cecily came to America?"

"Poor Whitmore died not too long after; she was only thirty-eight or so when she died. Hodgkin's disease. They seem to have written when they were apart, but one gathers that wasn't often. We also have Cecily's letters, which were returned to her at Whitmore's death. Perhaps a dozen each way."

"Soon I'll throw myself upon your mercies and ask to look at them, just to see what they would have been for the student I mentioned. But now I'll cuddle up with the autobiography, if I may?"

"Certainly. Perhaps you can confirm me in my opinion that it's a rare piece, and worthy of publication. I leave you to it."

Kate found herself alone, in the silent room, with what was clearly the sketch for an autobiography. Yet as Sparrow had said, through the bare facts there seemed to escape the sense of what life must have been to Cecily, from the earliest days to the last. One could not put one's finger upon a single startling statement, yet one had the sense of enormous passion moving beneath the clear-cut words. Kate thought of Eliot's lines:

And what the dead had no speech for, when living,
They can tell you, being dead: the communication
Of the dead is tongued with fire beyond the language
    of the living.

Here certainly the reverberations owed something to the fact that the woman writing was now dead. Kate, finishing the fragment, went back to the beginning to account for the sense of vividness left with her. The stages of Cecily's life were clear enough.

She had been born in 1900, the child of a middle-aged lecturer at a Welsh university who had, after the death of his first wife, married a student, brilliant and with that peculiar grace people seem unable to describe without allusions to wild and frightened colts. The sons of Hutchins' first marriage had grown and departed, grateful to the young wife for removing, from their consciences and lives, the aching loneliness of their father. Cecily was her parents' only child, and both of them treated her as though she were a magic being who might, if roughly treated, dematerialize. She was, as she was to remain, frail, slender to the point of spindliness, but with a vigor, a love of movement, particularly walking and swimming, which she was to keep till the last. Her childhood companions, when she was not with adults, as is the inevitable lot of the only child, were two neighbor boys whose lack of masculine exclusiveness neatly met what was considered, in her case, excessive wildness in female form. She learned early to keep her adventures to herself, and a spare set of old clothes in the garden shed. Whatever ladylike attitudes she may have assumed for the sake of her parents and their circle, she never doubted that to be a boy was to have won the better part. When it was borne in upon her, well and truly, with the departure of her neighbors for their public school, that no amount of disguise or persuasion could make her eligible for a life in the Navy—clearly, were one free to choose, the ideal existence—she became nervous, a great reader, and a grudging figure at her mother's tea parties.

Fortunately at this time she came to the notice of her Aunt Mary—her mother's sister—who had worked with Harriet Weaver and Rebecca West on *The New Free-woman*, soon to become *The Egoist*. Aunt Mary had known Ezra Pound, and Richard Aldington and H.D. and their group, and had earlier decided to devote her life to service in the general hospital staffed entirely by women doctors and serving women patients only, which had opened in the early years of the century. Aunt Mary offered to send Cecily to Oxford. There Cecily flourished, having made that delightful discovery which Forster was later to claim as the special provenance of Cambridge—that there are people in the world with interests like one's own, people who do not care what "they" think. The Oxford years, just after the war, were the watershed for her; after them, companionships and intellectual excitement were possible. Cecily, scarcely down from Oxford, established herself as a fashionable and erudite novelist. Her sparkling novels—"brittle" to those of a sentimental or conventional turn of mind—were notable for featuring as protagonist a woman of enormous dispassion whose experiences seemed to arise from her physical vigor and vigorous rationality, which between them neatly, and of course wittily, encompassed the passionate. Cecily herself, presented by her doctor aunt with a minuscule flat, began to live, in the midst of London, a life filled with parties, clever conversation, and much scintillating accomplishment. She was the valued companion of everyone in England's family life of literature and was marvelously, preposterously happy. Her dispassion protected her from doctrinaire Communism, her rationality from Fascism, and her wit from the religious conversion which seemed inevitable for all the most humanist and Bloomsburyish of her acquaintances. She shared this life, and the minuscule flat, with Dorothy Whitmore.

Then, late in the 1920s, she met, fell passionately in love with, and, like a woman in a dream, married Ferdinand Ricardo, an already famous painter whose past was somewhere in Europe and whose future was to be in America. Somehow, soon after their marriage, his name became simply Ricardo, as Colette's had become Colette. Their adventures after the move to America were not told, perhaps because Cecily's spirit had not partaken of them. Eventually, in search of solitude, Cecily built the house by the sea and lived there with Ricardo, who was now old and settled. Somewhere in those late years, the spirit returned.

After Ricardo died, she wrote *A Lonely Place*. It had been solitude Cecily sought, but she had learned that one must woo solitude under its harsher name of loneliness. With an irony typical of the United States, Cecily Hutchins, in revealing her own daily wrestle with loneliness, as a widow and writer, touched so mightily upon the loneliness of others that the loneliness and its sister, solitude, became imperiled. *A Lonely Place* brought her fame, of the sort she did not want (though, Kate thought, it would help sell Max's biography), and money, which she did not especially need. She resisted easily enough the television offers, the huge sums for columns in the women's magazines. She also resisted, less easily, Kate surmised, the temptation to look for encouragement in one's new work to critics, friends, editors. Alone, she wrote at the age of seventy-three her best novel, and lived to see it acclaimed, a privilege denied, Kate thought, to Dorothy Whitmore.

The whole was a success story, and no doubt would itself achieve success. The form was almost classic—the move from early to late solitude, both imposed, both welcome. It occurred to Kate, leaning back in her wooden chair with the high back, the manuscript might be a success these days for another reason. Cecily had achieved a portrait of a women's life that was not, for all its domesticity, essentially domestic. Her children did not seem to invite much discussion or comment. Her passion for Ricardo, her marriage, became the center of her life only as these could be transformed into a relationship able to thrive on separation and independence. Altogether, quite a modern document.

Kate carefully returned the manuscript to its folder, gathered up her belongings, and went in search of Sparrow. She found him in his office grappling with proofs for programs and plans for an exhibition.

"I did glance through the Whitmore letters, since you seemed so fascinated," he said to Kate. "They're not especially interesting. It seems to have been one of those relationships where the two said a great deal to each other, and wrote only perfunctory notes when apart. It's quite common."

"Or the reverse," Kate said. "I have a friend—we were at college together—with whom I maintain a really exciting correspondence. But whenever we meet we discuss her children and my teaching schedule. Thank you, Mr. Sparrow, for a fine day."

"Thank you for a fine lunch. We will meet again soon, I hope." He walked Kate to the elevator, as though a lady might not be counted upon to muster the strength to press the button or because—and Kate had noticed this at other men's clubs—the members seemed vaguely to feel that an unaccompanied woman might get loose and not be found for days, only to reappear suddenly and frighten the inmates. Here at least Sparrow trusted her to reach the ground floor in safety, where another ancient black man of the same age and vintage as the first bowed her out the door.

It is good for the soul, Kate thought to herself, hailing a taxi, to make an occasional foray into a statelier era.

part three

{ May }

eight

The first week of May, and the last week of classes at the university; Kate had written Phyllis to expect her on the eighth of May. Meanwhile, life in May, as was its yearly habit for those connected with the academic world, intensified perceptively over life in April—or March, or February. At the university, there were papers: course papers, master's essays, chapters of doctoral dissertations, all flowering as though they were daffodils, or did she mean tulips? Kate was always vague about botanic allusions. All Kate really knew about daffodils, apart from Wordsworth's rather hysterical admiration of them, was that they came before the swallow dared. Just *when* the swallow dared was another unknown . . . like everything else in my life, Kate gloomily thought.

"The one advantage to my existence," Kate had recently remarked to Reed, "is that there are so many different problems I never spend long enough on one to become quite catatonic." The trouble with successful businessmen, for example, she thought now, was that they never really concentrated on anything else, never actually focused all their attention elsewhere. They liked recreation and dalliance to be sure, but this was to relieve the tension of business worries, not to substitute one serious matter for another. Can that be what I've always disliked about businessmen? Kate asked herself. Or is the prejudice just a grumbling response to my impossible family.

This thought brought her, of course, to Leo. In one moment, she would have to go down the hall to a committee meeting; ten minutes ago she had come from a class. Now she sat in her office and, guiltily, removed the phone from the hook. She wanted a moment to think. Of Leo, of Gerry Marston. Of England.

"The trouble with him," Leo had once remarked to her of someone, "is that he hasn't got his act together." Leo was full of these phrases, clichés of his generation, most of them indicating a lack of integration. Small wonder. Kate remembered that Leo had once responded, when asked his opinion of a dinner guest: "I don't know where he's coming from." Kate thought that both phrases described her rather well at the moment, or at least various puzzles in her life. Yet she had to admit, to herself at least, that since Max's appearance in her cabin, and Leo's wrestle with dishonor, she felt more alive, better: quite simply, less in despair. Was one so dependent on outer stimulation as that?

The point, shorn of its niceties, was that we all want to feel a part of something ongoing. Could the death of poor Gerry, or the cheating of Ricardo, be called ongoing? Some of us, she thought, spend our lives in preparation for what will probably never happen; others, like me, only live in a state of alarmed, but vital, unpreparedness. What with Leo, the Wallingford, university work, and the hours of end-of-semester student conferences, she had not been to the cabin in weeks.

I must go there, she thought, after England, and work all this out. I'm in a muddle.

Whenever she sat in the office, which was rarely, quiet and barricaded (door shut, light out, phone off the hook), she thought of Gerry Marston, gentle, helpful, twenty-three—a girl who knew what she wanted from life, knew, at least, in what center of herself resided the possibilities of work and love (which Freud, with that rare simplicity achieved by the great, had called the important things in life). She was dead, and Kate longed, with a fervor as potent as it was irrational, to discover, somehow, why she had died, and how. But what else was there to do? In detective novels, which Kate had found herself reading less and less with the passing years, the detective would set out to discover. All sorts of other things would then happen, leading to one suspected criminal after another, not to mention other murders, attempted or achieved. (Kate thought particularly of Dick Francis, whose books she still did read, because she liked him and to discover how he would work the horses in this time.) In life, they simply removed a body from the rocks, and one's nephew became closely involved in the modern world of violence, vandalism, cheating, and success which had nothing to do with accomplishment. One, meanwhile, remembering always the body in the pool between the rocks, went off to England to see if Somerville College had changed in fifty years.

There was a knock on the door. Kate opened it, to find Evergreen. "Coming to the meeting?" he said. His office was next to hers. "I'll be right along," Kate answered, smiling and closing the door so that he would not see the phone off the hook, about which she felt idiotically guilty. The lack of light, so that none could be seen through the glass top of the door, revealing one's presence within, was a trick practiced by all who could think, or write, in the dark. One of the Renaissance professors, who could not, had put up a shade on the inside of his door, so that no one could tell if the light was on or not: ingenious.

Kate replaced the phone on the hook, and immediately it rang. The caller was Max.

"Ah. I had about concluded that you were engaged in the reorganization of the university with the president himself."

"Not bloody likely; though I do admit, if he asked me for suggestions I could go on for days. How are you, Max?"

"Fine, except that my struggles with Cecily's family over her papers having finally resolved themselves, I now appear to be caught up in some crisis with a Ricardo son; something to do with cheating, or accusations thereof. Do I remember your mentioning, at our lovely luncheon at the Cos Club, that your nephew and the Ricardo boy were buddies? Or is the word chums? Friends I could scarcely hope for."

"None of those things. Enemies would probably be closer to it." Kate did not remember Max as having been so skittish before, and she found she didn't care for it.

"Oh, dear, oh, dear. Do you know what the trouble is all about? I'm afraid the Ricardo version is a bit vague."

"Ricardo got someone to take the SAT for him," Kate said. "You were, I now remember, surprised at his having got into Harvard."

"But surely that's impossible. Don't they police those exams?"

"Only in a totally inadequate way. Incidentally"— Kate thought suddenly, for reasons not far to seek, of taped telephone conversations—"I should have said that it is *alleged*—I believe that is the legal term—that someone else took the exam for him."

Max was clearly shaken. "I find it difficult to believe anyone would do such a thing. Still, these days . . ." His voice trailed off.

"Did you want something from me?" Kate asked, in what she hoped were not too abrupt tones. She was already five minutes late to the committee meeting.

"Just to have you hold my hand, as always. I do seem to throw myself upon your mercies at every crisis. Or perhaps only at the Ricardo-connected ones. The family, that is Cecily's children, thought that I might do something since I have what they are fond of referring to as academic connections."

"What could you do?"

"Obviously nothing. A most disturbing business. The boy, of course, denies the whole thing. You will let me know if you hear any more, won't you? Having just got myself set straight with these people, I hate to plunge *immediately* into another muddle, particularly one I can't seem to do anything about."

"It's just a mark of the times," Kate said. "Everyone cheats these days. When were there paper-writing agencies? One can't even be sure one's master's essays are written by the student any more."

"*I* can be sure. It's all because of a lack of discipline, student rioting, a loss of all values. Dear me."

That's just what Nixon would have said, Kate

thought. "I must go now, Max. I'm off to England in a few days, but I'll be in touch when I get back."

"Thank God you didn't say you'd contact me. I look forward to your return, Kate. Goodbye."

I'm sure Nixon used "contact" as a verb all the time, Kate thought, walking down the corridor to her meeting. And that knowledge gave her, for no reason she could discern, much relief.

"Did everybody always suppose his or her world to be crumbling to pieces?" Kate asked that night, lying on the couch in the living room. Reed sat at the piano, picking out tunes from the twenties, in an idle, undistracting way.

"I'm sure they did," he answered. "They were just more grandiloquent about it; think of Euripides and the Trojan women. Besides, we're getting near the end of the century. *Fin de siècle*, and all that."

" '*Fin de globe*,' Wilde said."

"There you are, then."

"I remember," Kate said, "Clarence Day, or perhaps it was J. P. Marquand, writing about his father's coming out of his house to see the man next door on the stoop of his house in his shirtsleeves. He immediately concluded the neighborhood was deteriorating, and put his house on the market. Clarence Day's father did, I mean, or J. P. Marquand's. The signals were subtler in those days, and less devastating."

Reed modulated nicely from "Smoke Gets in Your Eyes" to Coward's "A Room with a View." "What do you make of that Finlay boy?" he asked, neatly achieving a diminished seventh as accompaniment; Reed's chords were apt to be sparse and dubiously chosen.

"As a studier of the young, I would say right off that he was a clear case of someone longing to be caught and relieved of burdens of guilt. After all, why tell everyone in your class else? All he had to do was shut up, and nothing in the world would have happened. Even Leo and his righteous friends would have let it go without a murmur, I'm sure, if it hadn't been a question of the school knowing."

"I'm sure you're right," Reed said, finishing with a series of chords and swinging around to face the other way on the piano bench. "At least as far as you go. Why in the world he wanted to do any such thing to have burdens of guilt about is another matter. He had it made. Not only rich, and blond, and tall, and a champion wrestler, *and* generally charming, but a genius into the bargain—or, to modulate Leo's term, a damn gifted boy able to use all he had. And with a family reaching back through generations of social accomplishment."

"The way you put it, it all does sound rather awful, in the true sense of the word. Maybe he just had to make something go wrong, before something went wrong from the outside, if you see what I mean?"

"I see, but that's to make him sound rather like you, if you don't mind my mentioning it. Leo's version is that he had the idea he could control anything, including getting his friend into college. Why should my friend not go to Harvard because of those tests?—that sort of thing."

"And in Ricardo he found, of course, the perfect lad to take exams on behalf of. Leo says Ricardo drives without a license, not seeing why he should bother with such mundane matters if he wants to get somewhere. All that occasionally restrains him, one gathers, is the knowledge that if caught he won't be allowed to get a license for five years. He's like that manager who told his pitcher to hit the fellow on the other team with a bean ball, or is my mind wandering? Everything is all right for me to do, because my side is the right side."

"That is the sickening aspect of this whole affair, if you'll permit me to ignore the reference to bean balls, which sounds exclusive and athletic. The criminal mind at its simplest and best, but now shared by everyone. Since my cause is right—whatever it may be, anything from the presidency of the United States to a business deal or the pressure that makes it excusable to go through a red light—whatever my cause, my disdain for the law is justified. Disdain for the law on the part of others, nonetheless, is an insult to America and must be prevented." Reed swung back to face the piano, and began to accompany himself: "The words you are speaking you were speaking then, but I can't remember where or when."

"Ricardo does have a point, however. He says if a Kennedy can get into Harvard because he's a Kennedy, and some other moron because his father gave the money for the new hockey rink, why shouldn't he use what pull he has, meaning Finlay taking the tests for him?"

"I'm surprised at you, Kate. We are none of us born equal, however created. There is a difference between using the advantages one has because of one's birth, and cheating to get honors one does not deserve by any standard. After all, even the Kennedys have paid, and continue to pay, a pretty stiff price for all their advantages. So does the rich kid whose father built the hockey rink. One might as well say Leo shouldn't have got into college because he did well on the verbal SAT through living with a glib aunt of large and distinguished vocabulary. Anyway, I gather the Ricardo boy is very smooth—cool is Leo's word—which doesn't sound as though he's particularly concerned with social justice as a principle."

"Do you think it possible the Ricardo boy could be at all like Max? Or do I mean Finlay? After all, neither is any real relation. Max called me today about the St. Anthony's drama, by the way, so my two problems are merging. The dead girl who was honorable, and the live boy who was not."

"My advice," Reed said, "is to have a nightcap, and try to concentrate on England, not on puzzles. Think of Phyllis, for a short time able to enjoy your company, no longer doomed to stroll alone and aimlessly down the High, or is it up?"

Kate promised to think about England as ordered.

The promise was more easily kept the next day, when she found on her desk a letter from Crackthorne.

"Extraordinary to report," he wrote, "I miss the basketball games and our lively, if unaudible, conversations. I am, however, writing you for selfish and grasping reasons which must not be camouflaged by sighs of regret. Rumor hath it that the Wallingford has the Cecily Hutchins papers, and that you are as near as any female can be to membership in that august body. Is there any chance that a mere dissertation writer, however given to male athletics, might have a look? She might have mentioned or corresponded with some of my chaps. I mean, there they all were, and

123

maybe some who returned from or lived through the war spoke to her or, delicious hope, wrote to her."

Ah, Kate thought, two can play at this game. She dashed off a note to Crackthorne asking him to notice if Hutchins, Whitmore, or any of that generation of women turned up in the course of *his* research. She pleased herself considerably by announcing to him that she would be in Oxford one week hence, and giving him her address should he have learned anything worth communicating.

She then opened her door to announce to those waiting outside the commencement of her office hour. It annoyed Kate to discover, sometime later, how to heart she had taken Reed's advice to think about England, and all its ramifications. Especially its ramifications. Kate usually enjoyed her office hours, but today her thoughts kept slipping away to the Wallingford, and she would recall herself from a reverie to find she had missed at least two rambling paragraphs of a student's problems. Eventually Kate gave it up and put in a call to Sparrow, begging to be allowed to come down for another look.

"I won't make a habit of it and take advantage of your generosity," she promised. "But it turns out I shall soon be going to England, and I want to make some sense of it all. I suspect I merely want to commune," she weakly concluded. The fact is, she told herself in a taxi on the way east, I envy Max. I would like to write the biography. My motives are impure to a degree. Drag the disgraceful fact out into the open and face it, Kate Fansler. However good Max may be, a woman ought to write that biography. A thoroughly sexist

124

remark, she concluded, paying off the driver and greeting the dignified doorman as to the manner born.

"We haven't got a bit further with sorting," Sparrow said, as they faced the boxes. "But commune away. When you've finished, root me out and let's have a sherry—after the official closing, that is. You will put everything back?"

"I'll be good," Kate said. "Trust me." And indeed, he was good, too. She felt, however, a bit sneaky at not having rung up Max to say she was coming. Well, Cecily, she thought, here we are. What remains of a life?

What chiefly remained stood between bookends on a table in the center of the room. Cecily's books, the first edition of each bought by the Wallingford as part of the "papers." There were twenty of them, a goodly number considering the care with which she wrote. She remembered Max long ago remarking of some extremely popular woman writer that she wrote more novels in a year than he read. Still, it was amazing what even so careful an artist as Cecily could produce by working steadily for a few hours every day. Kate turned resolutely from the novels. It had occurred to her during the night that the Bodleian was a depository, which meant that a copy of every book published in England was placed there. Since the library was noncirculating, it supposedly remained there, unlike the books in the library of Kate's university, which circulated so steadily in ever-widening circles that one's chances of finding any given book were fifty-fifty at best. Sitting in the Bodleian, between bouts of reviving Phyllis and the nostalgic rediscovery of the Oxford scene, she could read her way through the entire canon of Cecily *and* of Dorothy Whitmore if it came to that.

Was there anything rational to be expected of the papers at this point? The boxes were marked with their contents, and one box was labeled "Unclassified." These, Kate discovered, were the papers actually on Cecily's desk at the time of her death, including, oddly enough, unopened letters. Supposedly these had accumulated at the post office during her absence in England, and had been returned to the house after her death. How odd, however, that they had not been opened. Suppose they had required an answer? But looking through them, Kate saw they were all personal letters from correspondents known or unknown; the bills and other business matters had been dealt with by the lawyer or the children. These, supposed to be literary, had, she gathered, been left for Max. Kate picked them up and shuffled through them idly; then she stopped. There was a letter from Gerry Marston. Typed, in a long white envelope, with Gerry's return address (her room at the university) in the upper left-hand corner. The postmark was hard to read, the date unclear, as was more and more likely these days.

Kate boldly carried the letter in to Sparrow. "I suppose there is no chance that we can open this?"

Sparrow stared at it. "Yes," he said. "I take it that is your student, whom Max mentioned died in Maine. Odd no one noticed it before now."

"No doubt it was shuffled in with all the other letters that looked as though they came from readers, individuals rather than firms."

"Well," Sparrow said, "it does belong to the Walling-

126

ford. Still . . . what do you say if I call Max and ask if we can open it?"

"A brilliant suggestion, if only he is there."

He was there. Apparently he was murmuring his apologies for leaving the letters this long, and said that of course Kate might open it. So Sparrow reported. Taking a long letter opener, he slit the envelope neatly across the top, drew out the typewritten sheet, and handed it to Kate. She, responding to his courtesy, read it aloud:

" 'Dear Miss Hutchins: Thank you for your kind and prompt reply. I am disappointed to hear that you have nothing of great importance in connection with my work on Dorothy Whitmore, but I am excited to hear of the portrait. You are kind to invite me to visit you and see it when you return from England, and I look forward greatly to hearing from you then. Thank you also for saying you will make a search for anything you might have on Whitmore, even if you are so certain there is nothing. Sincerely yours,' and it's signed 'Geraldine Marston.' "

"But supposedly she decided not to wait for Cecily's return and went in for a little housebreaking?" Sparrow said, after a pause.

"It must have been almost maddening to have to sit on her hands and do nothing. I doubt she went in for housebreaking. She probably decided it would do no harm to survey the landscape, so to speak, and the landscape unfortunately included those rocks. I don't suppose I could make a copy of this letter?"

"Of course no copy can be made," Sparrow sternly said. "Those are the terms of the purchase. What you need," he added, "is a glass of sherry. Excuse me while

I get it." And he walked from the room, stopping as he went to tap his fingers on some machine near the door. Some machine. It was—by God, it was a copying machine. Kate was used to them; who, in these benighted times, was not? They were almost as ubiquitous as the internal combustion engine. Within seconds Kate had a copy of the letter in her purse, the original was back on Sparrow's desk, and she was staring vaguely from the window when he returned. Sparrow poured the sherry.

"To your trip," he said, raising his glass. "I envy you."

128

nine

An English writer, himself a graduate of Cambridge, remarked years ago in his autobiography that "every Oxonian has at least one book about Oxford inside him, and generally gets it out." Nobody who has been to Cambridge, he claimed, feels compelled to write about it. This generality, while untrue, had, like so many generalities, enough truth about it to make it stick. Certainly Kate, standing in front of the Martyrs Memorial, was inclined to credit the assertion. Oxford seemed less her own memories than those of all the famous or merely accomplished people whose accounts of their time here, by themselves or others, she had read. (Not to mention the re-creations in fiction by those who had been unable to forget the dreaming spires.) Kate had, in her day, punted on the Cam, walked along the backs at Cambridge, and indulged, not always religiously, in reverence in Kings College Chapel. Certainly Cambridge's beauty was great. But for her Oxford was the hub of the scholar's universe, not least because, an industrial city, it was a place of secrets. Each of the colleges had courts and gardens unfolding, one from the other, known only to the initiated and often open only to the invited. Kate wondered what life in an American university would be like if each group of faculty had a beautiful "fellows" garden in which to converse and behold nature in the form of a carefully tended flower bed and an ancient tree. But if the flowers in the college gardens grew more beautifully than ever, the buildings and traffic beyond prevented any sense that Oxford was in a state of static preservation. Blackwell's shipping building on Parkend Street, however ancient their store across from the Sheldonian, was all glass and air conditioning and looked as though it had been designed for downtown Detroit. At least, Kate comforted herself, enough sense had prevailed to prevent tall buildings; the spires still dominated the sky, including the atrocious one in Nuffield, built in 1958 to house a library, with no sense of either fitness or discretion.

Kate walked round to retrieve her just-rented bicycle from the rack behind the monument. She had brought her detestation of the motorcar with her into a city likely to be choked by automobiles; she planned to pedal around Oxford in what she hoped was a properly eccentric manner. Kate, bearing to the left, signaled her intention to turn into St. Giles, thence into the Woodstock Road and past the entrance to Somerville, where Cecily and Dorothy Whitmore and Max's mother were soon to begin their new friendship.

In fact, Kate's research had extended far enough* for her to know that in 1918 Somervillians were still being housed in the St. Mary Hall Quadrangle of Oriel College, the usual male inhabitants of these sacred precincts having gone to be slaughtered at Ypres and

* Chiefly in Vera Brittain, *The Women at Oxford*, London: Harrap, 1960.

Neuve Chapelle. Somerville College, next to the Radcliffe Infirmary, had been commandeered for conversion into a military hospital, while, at St. Mary Hall, the connecting hall between the men's living quarters and the women's had been bricked up. According to Oxford legend, some intrepid souls from either side (or both) had removed the bricks, and until they could be replaced, the Principal of Somerville guarded her side of the gap, the Provost of Oriel his.

Kate passed Somerville, not without a soulful look, which nearly cost her dearly as some truck lurched out from the Radcliffe Infirmary. By the time Somerville was again a college, in 1919, Whitmore and Hutchins were in their second year. Whitmore, who had served two years with the British Army, was the older. Pondering on this, Kate passed the Observatory, neatly missed turning down into Observatory Street—Phyllis had been very explicit about this—passed the small block of stores on the Woodstock Road—Kate ticked them off in her mind: a drugstore (chemists to the residents), a cleaners, a grocery, a shop that sold postcards and the like—and turned left into St. Bernard's Road. Phyllis's house was on the left, about a third of the way down, recognizable, Phyllis had said, by having the only uncut grass, front and back, on the street. "One is *very* frowned upon." Kate set her bicycle against the railings, and locked it to them with the chain provided by the bicycle people. Had one always needed to lock bicycles in Oxford? She rang the bell.

"What you need," Phyllis said, "is a drink. Welcome to the shabbiest living room in Oxford, and that's saying a good deal. No, don't sit on that couch, you will

131

sink through to the floor and end up in the lotus position. Whenever I look at that couch, I am reminded of that bit from *Private Lives* where the current wife announces that she is so shocked at Elyot's running off with Amanda that she feels as though slimy things had been crawling all over her, and Elyot says: 'Maybe they have, that's a very old sofa.' That chair is ugly, commodious, and surprisingly comfortable. Kate, I don't remember when I've been so glad to see anyone. Now I shall stop burbling on and say how are you? How are you? Scotch all right? We have a refrigerator designed to hold one orchid for one social butterfly; there's room for little else. But in joy at the thought of your arrival, I have managed the production of two ice cubes. After the first drink, you can sip your whisky warm, in the way that built and lost the empire. I'll be right back. The kitchen, needless to say, is down a flight of steep stairs, which debouch directly into the privy."

Kate, happily sunk into the ugly and commodious chair, thought that if one could not have been at Oxford in 1920 with Whitmore for a friend, one was fairly lucky to be there over half a century later with Phyllis for a friend. Even in such a room as this. For its shabbiness was indeed of a magnificent degree, as though thousands of Leos had flung themselves against the springs and wiped their feet upon the slipcovers. Filling the fireplace was a gas heater whose efficiency must have been great to compensate for such atrocity of appearance. In the corner stood a television set. On the floor was a rug whose reason for existence must have been warmth; it could not have been aesthetic. Yet, Kate happily thought, it was a marvelous room for conversation, for its only furniture were two overstuffed couches and two overstuffed chairs, and one dim standing lamp in the corner. Since Phyllis was not poor, the house must have been chosen for reasons having nothing to do with its furniture.

Her joy at Kate's arrival in Oxford had been touching, however expected. Phyllis had once, she had told Kate on the phone, read a book by an American wife of a visiting professor to Oxford entitled *These Ruins Are Inhabited,* and, she had said, if the title hadn't been used she would be prepared to write the book herself. Since she shared Kate's besotted Anglophilia, they were, so to speak, ripe for the exchange of impressions.

"Dieu que la vie est quotidienne," Phyllis remarked, returning with two stiff drinks, one with ice. "Laforgue would have known what of he spoke if he'd ever been in Oxford in term time while unconnected with any aspect of the university. You can't imagine. One trots to a series of little stores for one's food, bread here, meat there, salad in a third place, everyone as pleasant as can be, of course, that's what makes it possible, the English shopkeepers are so pleasant, not like those in New York, who seem to conclude you've entered the store for the express purpose of being insulted. Still, it does wear. Sometimes I go down to the Oxford market and wait on long, serpentine lines at Palme's for really good cheese and bread, but mostly I go to Marks and Spencer and buy prepared shepherd's pie. Hugh grumbles a bit, but he's always being invited out to elegant meals in hall somewhere, and even he admits no one less domestic than a Victorian cook could function in that kitchen. The height of my week is the visit to the laundromat. One goes either at night, when one meets

undergraduates, or during the day, when one meets the wives of young dons. The company is better at night. Those wives. I can't imagine how England ever assimilated Germaine Greer; I've never seen a place where women are such slaves. Of course, the American wives who visit are little better; look at me. Well, you, dear Kate, are a marvelous change. You will, I know, be infinitely relieved to learn that I am taking you out to dinner. Now, what is this old history you're digging up, and why, and how is Reed?"

"Reed is fine. The other questions will take a little longer, and a bit more whisky. Phyllis, how in the world did you manage to acquire this extraordinary house?"

Phyllis chuckled. "I respond like the Vassar girl who was asked how she ended up a prostitute: pure luck. It's the bathrooms that did it, plus the incredible shortage of housing in Oxford in term time. Hugh, it goes without saying, didn't make up his mind to spend a year at the Clarendon until we were practically on our way to the airport, and this came up for rent suddenly. Someone must have collapsed at simple contemplation of all the stairs. All I knew about it was that it had three johns and two bathrooms. The other house we might have had had a privy on the bottom floor minus one, so to speak, a bathroom-minus-privy on the third floor, and one slept, fitfully I'm sure, on the top. I'm just American enough to be unable to do without a bathroom to myself, though, as you can see, I do without most other amenities. I *think* the lady who owns this intended originally to have flats, which is why so many bathrooms. The English, I've decided, go in the morning when they get up and never again. You wouldn't expect it with all that tea, but no doubt their bladders are trained from birth. Also, there's a fairly good heating system, which is to say a glassful of water will not actually turn to ice if left in here overnight, and there's plenty of hot water, which is grand, until one discovers that it's produced by some incredible submersion heater that works with the noise of a jet engine and costs the earth to run. We've four floors, two rooms on a floor, which is convenient if one has guests; one can isolate them in layers. Hugh says it's a vertical ranch house. Since I can't resist the marvelous English beer in the marvelous pubs, it's nice to know I take it all off puffing up stairs all day. And that's why I'm here. Actually, this is a sort of interstitial street: dons began to live here when dons could marry, at the Woodstock end, that is. The working class lives at the Walton end. The new construction is housing for St. John's, so no doubt St. Bernard's Road is coming up in the world. Now, your turn. Produce your explanation and pray make it improbable."

Kate kicked off her shoes and tucked her feet under her on the chair. The absence of tables was partly explained by the ease with which one could balance a glass on the wide arms of the ancient chairs. She had read in a book that Colette, whom Kate enormously admired, had said that friendship, like love, naturally speaks its true language only in a duet. It occurred to her that one of the problems she had begun to encounter in recent years arose from the impossibility of such conversations in the ordinary routine of life. Everyone was either too busy, if they were worth talking to, or too dull, if they were available. She had, to recover herself, chosen occasional solitude in the

135

cabin Reed had given her in lieu, perhaps, of friendship. Or, once past youth, did one find one's conversations, if any, only with those with overlapping interests or those met by serendipity, in foreign parts, both of you orbiting outside the usual gravitational forces, like Phyllis? She asked the question.

"You," said Phyllis, "are growing to resemble a psychiatrist or a Jewish comedian, always answering a question with a question. Of course, I know just what you mean. I've never been lonelier in my life, and I, unlike you, haven't newly discovered writers to think about. My major aim in life, I shall confess to you, is to eat in one of those halls in the men's colleges. Hugh says that that's still impossible, and even if he got me invited to one of those colleges that admit women exist—because I am a professional, actually head of a school on a year's leave, though no one ever seems to remember it here, or care—it would all be immensely strained and lonely. The poor dear dons haven't eaten with women in so long, Hugh says, they would think the food was tainted. Either they're bachelors and live in college, or they're married men who leave their poor wives and children home for a supper of corn flakes, and arrive in hall to dine elegantly and with proper service. One of the perks for dons, you know, is a full and elaborate dinner. All that was written into the rules before dons married. I think with what relief they leave the domestic scene and repair to their safe masculine precincts. Which are in danger, I'm glad to report, of being no longer safe. Some colleges, like Exeter, I think, have never had a woman in hall and claim they never will. Not that the dear English are all that welcoming even to *male* visitors. Some prominent male American professors have been known to die of social chills. Nonetheless, damn it, I still admire the trees and gardens and lawns this side of idolatry. Sometimes I go to look at the deer at Magdalen and think that they brought them there to make the boys from large estates feel at home, and that probably the descendants of those boys think that women ought to be kept in more or less the same attractive and confined way. That world is over, but it had its beauty."

"What a beauty," Kate sighed. "Imagine life in the nineteen twenties when there were still rules about mixed parties and, as L. P. Hartley said, hope took for granted what in these days fear takes for granted. Phyllis, if I utter one more word of nostalgia, hit me."

"I'll hit you with another Scotch," Phyllis said. She returned with the bottle, no more ice being, as she had explained, available, and placed the bottle on the floor between them. Kate poured herself another drink. "What I don't understand," Phyllis said, "is what you're doing here, besides rescuing me. Ought I to have heard of Dorothy Whitmore?"

"Not really. We were both too young to see the movie they made of her novel; she was a good friend of Cecily Hutchins. In fact, I'd better make a clean breast of it—where in the world did that expression come from, do you imagine?—and tell you the whole story. Have you met Max Reston?"

"Have I not? He knows Hugh through his brother, Reston's, I mean, and now and then he turns up at the Cosmopolitan Club, Reston, I mean, not his brother."

"He turned up there recently with me, as a matter of fact, but that was later. It began in March when I was up at the cottage Reed gave me. But of course, I haven't told you about that. I'm beginning to sound like my oldest sister-in-law, who is always going so far back to explain all the elements in every story that I begin to wonder if she is dull on purpose; one couldn't, I sometimes feel, be that boring by accident."

"You're not boring me. I've only learned to know the meaning of boredom these last months."

Kate ended up telling the story, in almost sister-in-law detail, as she thought of it. She concluded with an admission of her profound excitement at the thought of reading Whitmore's letters, which she had already established were in the Somerville library. "Whitmore left her letters to Max's mother, who left them to Somerville. I long to read them, of course on my way to visit you. How fortunate your situation is for Whitmore research." This brought her back to Gerry Marston. Kate's tale was, as tales are with friends who understand conversation, full of digressions that eventually rejoined the main stream neatly, as in medieval literature.

"Are you suggesting," Phyllis asked, "that Max killed her?"

"No, of course not. At least, I don't think so. Max might freeze someone to death with disdain, but violence isn't his style. Even if he had the smallest reason for killing her, which he hasn't. Max is a true gentleman in that he is never rude unintentionally, but surely not even his withering intentions reach as far as mayhem. But it all does seem odd. And it's left me with a hunger to know more of Whitmore and Hutchins. Phyllis, do we have to go out? Couldn't we have a Marks and Spencer shepherd's pie here and get beautifully sozzled?"

"Why not. I've even got some beer, in returnable bottles, bless the English. I'll go and light the oven now, so that we can eat in three hours. The explosion you are about to hear is part of the scenario, and should not be regarded in the light of a catastrophe."

When she came back soon, no sound of an explosion having intervened, it was to announce that she had been inspired. "We shan't eat shepherd's pie and drink bottled beer, we'll walk along the river to Binsey and have cheese and pickle sandwiches in the garden of the Perch. Are you still the greatest walker as ever was?"

"Still. I remember the path, and the boats and swans."

"They're there yet," Phyllis assured her, "with the addition of much litter, here as the world over, alas. In England, needless to say, one cannot function without first memorizing opening and closing times—why should the English make life simple and let you drink whenever you feel like it? At least it gives a shape to my day. Ah, I say, I'll walk to the market and then, on the way back, the Lamb and Flag will have opened and I'll have a beer. Let's see; we've got time for one more drink and a wash and brush up; I do hope that's the correct English phrase—I keep trying to use them but always get them wrong, somehow. Hugh will be here when we return, and you can get the male side of life at Oxford from him. Believe me, compared to the lives of females not lucky enough to be attached somewhere, it's pure heaven, even if Hugh constantly complains that the English love of animals makes the use of even one laboratory mouse a matter of state.

Someone in Hugh's lab got called on the carpet for cruelty to shrimp, if you'll believe it."

They set off in a direction not usually recommended to those visitors invited to All Souls. They walked toward what Phyllis called the working-class end of St. Bernard's Road, past a pub which was apparently the local youth meeting place. Certainly neither the litter nor the noise suggested that English adolescents had anything over their American counterparts in neatness or discretion. "What Leo would like," Kate said, "is that in England one can, it seems, begin drinking beer before puberty. He's always asked to prove he's eighteen in the States, difficult, because he isn't."

They crossed Walton Street and continued down Walton Well Road. Almost immediately they were on the bridge over the railway tracks, with a clear view of a factory, product indeterminable, and then they were in the country. This quick transition from pavement to fields was, Kate always felt, close to the heart of England (whatever that meant), and she wondered how long England would be able to preserve it against the encroachments of suburbia and council housing. So far she had noticed that their town planning, like their broadcasting, was superior to America's, if their urban architecture was not. They crossed the river, passed through a gate, and were on the tow path to the Perch. This establishment was so picturesque, at least from the outside, that Kate began, as she always did at such moments, to wonder about the possibility of a job in England and a cottage nearby. Perhaps Phyllis, who had ended up on St. Bernard's Road beached on the shoals of boredom, had dreamed the same thing.

They went inside, which was rather more modern,

and found their cheese and pickle sandwiches, ordered a pint of beer each, and passed through a good deal of rather noisy conviviality into the garden. Here, as it happened, they were alone, possibly because the English drink indoors in a properly civilized manner. On the roof of the pub there rested, looking like something from a Blake drawing, two large white doves with fanlike tails.

"Not an hallucination," Phyllis said, following Kate's glance. "They live here. They're moulting or breeding or something sedentary at the moment, which is why they have that statuesque look. Hugh and I asked the owner about them not long ago. Well, Kate, here's to your adventure among the postwar Oxford generation. Keep me informed, will you? I feel like one of those dreary women who take up pottery or baking when the children start school, because there is no demand for their services from outside themselves. We always think we want life to be impromptu when we're middle-aged, but I expect I never meant as impromptu as all this." For a moment the boredom and depression showed forth from behind the glib talk.

"I shall certainly keep you informed," Kate said. "How about splitting another cheese and pickle?"

ten

So Kate settled down to read Whitmore's letters, sitting in one of the bays of the Somerville library looking out over the lawn-tennis courts and the great beech trees beyond. Kate was particularly intrigued with Whitmore's letters to her family from France, where she had served in the women's army corps. She had written stories at night by candlelight, and talked to the men for the fun of it. Of course, she had come back from the war thinking she could save the world. The League of Nations, and all that. She had been wrong; no one could save the world. But how wonderful, even for a short time, to have supposed that possible.

Kate, reading these letters and gazing out at the quadrangle, would picture it at an earlier time when Whitmore had come up in Michaelmas term, 1919. The following year, Whitmore's last, the statute giving women degrees came into force, and the first degree-giving ceremony in which women took part must have transformed the Sheldonian, Kate thought, into the sort of ceremony with which movie directors in the innocent days of Hollywood films used to end their pictures. In the words of Vera Brittain: "Inside the Sheldonian Theatre, its atmosphere tense with the consciousness of a dream fulfilled, younger and older spectators looked down . . . upon the complicated ceremony in the arena below. Then the great south doors opened and the five women principals, arrayed for the first time in caps and gowns, entered. . . . After a second's silence the theatre rang with unrehearsed applause, and the Vice-Chancellor rose to receive the first women Masters of Arts ever to appear in that historic place." In the world outside, Parliament had granted votes to women, thus freeing Oxford from the threat of appearing eccentric. In 1920, Kate thought, the new sight of women in scholars' and commoners' gowns whirling about the town on bicycles and running, as they are now, to the clamor of bells must have encouraged hope of progress. It must indeed have been a time of hope. And war, of course, was finished and would never return.

In the mornings, before Kate left the hotel for Somerville, her own letters would arrive. In this, too, England had clung, however precariously, to standards. They no longer had several deliveries a day; few even spoke now of the time when one could order from the grocer by postcard, and he would deliver your order the same day. But at least the mail arrived before nine o'clock in the morning, so that one started the day knowing where one was.

On the morning of the sixth day, Kate had three letters. She opened Reed's first. He assured her in his penultimate paragraph that the mess at St. Anthony's was progressing rather as expected. The faculty had been stunned by the news, not least of all, Reed suggested, because it had reached them through students. Their response had been varied and, as Reed had suspected, Leo and the other students had withstood

143

a certain amount of sharp remarks. This, Reed thought, would pass. She wasn't to worry. He was asking Leo to write.

Leo's letter, which Kate opened next, was remarkably reassuring, particularly since he did not mention the matter of the College Boards at all. He had apparently grasped that the purpose of his note was to reassure her that life was unchanged. "Dear Kate," he had written. "Everything fine here. Nothing special happening, though Reed said he would tell you what there is. I've been reading all the books I'm supposed to have read already for finals at the end of May. As you know, I took only bull shit courses my last term [by which, as he knew Kate knew, Leo meant literature courses]. In the midst of all your highbrow activities, why don't you go to see a professional soccer game. It's the great game all over Europe and South America, and you ought to see one, even if it isn't upper class. It's great to watch. Sit next to some man who'll explain the moves, if you can manage it. I'm sure you can. Love, Leo." Kate admired Leo's way of administering assurance, and the way he had moved onto the safe ground of athletics, even from afar.

Her third letter, a much fatter one, was from Crackthorne.

Dear Kate [he wrote], The end of the basketball season has left me with time for literary researches on your behalf; I reread a bit of Graves, and of course he was not only at Oxford with your crew, but at Somerville! Not that Whitmore, Hutchins, or any other female students are mentioned, but one certainly gets another view on the same life,

144

if that's what you're looking for. Needless to add, Somerville was a hospital when Graves was sent there before he was demobilized. They posted him for a time at Wadham to train officers, but the damp and hard work got the better of him, and he ended back at Somerville, where the men used to lounge around the grounds in their pajamas and dressing gowns, and even walk down St. Giles thus arrayed. What can Oxford have been coming to? But, as Graves points out, the social system had been dislocated. The don who was to be his moral tutor when he came up (the same time as your chaps, I think) was now a corporal and saluted Graves, who was a captain, every time they met. Aldous Huxley, of whom we were speaking at St. Anthony's great basketball victory, was there also, one of the few undergraduates in residence at the time. Graves used to visit Garsington, where everyone, but everyone, my dear, went, and where Clive Bell was passing the war looking after cows on the Garsington farm. All the CO's congregated there, apparently, because the Morrells were pacifists. But I must not get carried away with Graves's tales.

When Graves finally resigned his commission and came up to Oxford he was at St. John's college, but lived on Boar's Hill with all those other poets—I bet your trio visited there, if truth were told. What's more, Graves married a feminist who sounds rather amazingly up-to-date, actually, but must have seen pretty much eye-to-eye with Whitmore et al., shouldn't you think? Graves's wife kept her own name, was against religion ("God

145

is a man, so it must be all rot" was her unforgettable comment), and nearly refused to marry when she read the marriage service for the first time on their wedding day, just like the lady in Shaw's play. I wish Graves had actually mentioned your people, but he didn't apparently go back to Somerville after he came up, being too busy meeting T. E. Lawrence at All Souls, an anti-feminist place if ever one there was. I suppose all this is more worthy of conversation at a basketball game than as correspondence between two scholars, not to mention between a dissertation writer and his sponsor, but as you have no doubt gathered by now, frivolity is my long suit. Speaking of All Souls, Graves and Lawrence (T. E. again, D. H. being always committed to sterner and more important things) once planned to steal the Magdalen College deer and drive them into the small inner quadrangle of All Souls. The plan fell through, more's the pity, or the deer might have made it even if the women never did. Keep well, dear Kate, and send a postcard to your devoted friend and admirer, John Crackthorne.

Kate chuckled. Either Crackthorne had not heard of Leo's imbroglio, or he had decided to ignore it. Perhaps he did not think Kate knew about it yet; an overseas letter was scarcely the best medium for approaching so delicate a topic. Kate left the hotel and walked round to the back to fetch her bicycle, a form of transportation not usually employed by residents of Oxford's most expensive hotel, and looked upon by the employees thereof with a certain disdain, which was replaced by confusion at the size of her tips. It seemed to her pleasant to bicycle from her letters to Whitmore's, and she looked forward to tea that afternoon with Phyllis and Hugh.

"We can actually have tea, if you insist, as Hugh usually does," Phyllis had said, "but I'll have something with a bit more firmament on hand, should Hugh not appear." But Hugh did appear; this was the first time Kate had seen him in Oxford. He had not been there when they returned that night from Binsey. He greeted Kate with what for Hugh probably counted as effusion. (Kate thought instantly of Watson's description of his reunion with Holmes: "His manner was not effusive. It seldom was; but he was glad, I think, to see me.")

"You must forgive me, Kate," Hugh said, "and prove your forgiveness by letting me do something for you. Take you and Phyllis punting, to a cricket match, a boat race—what will it be?"

"Since you are so kind, sir," Kate answered, remembering Leo's letter, "I would like to see a professional soccer game."

"A what?" Phyllis asked.

"Oh, good heavens, Phyllis," Hugh said, "where have you been? It's all anybody talks about in a general way, but I didn't know people actually went to them. I thought they were dangerous and ended in riots and people beating each other over the head with the goal posts."

"Good," said Phyllis. "It sounds noisy and frightfully un-English. Let's go."

"Phyllis, my dear," Hugh said, helping himself to a muffin, "I don't know what's come over you this year. You never used to want to do something for the

147

wholly insufficient reason that I would rather you didn't."

"I know, poor Hugh, I know. I will abandon the soccer game," Phyllis said, sinking so far back upon the collapsible couch that her shoulders were on a level with her knees. "It's the hideously masculine quality of life here that's undoing me. Perhaps if a man lived at Oxford, unconnected with the university in any way, and married to a woman don, he, too, would suffer, and yet I doubt it, even if such a situation could be imagined. He'd be a writer, or a potterer in laboratories, or a bus driver, or *something*. You can't imagine how content the woman in England are to be slaves if they aren't actually professionals themselves."

Hugh chuckled, and as he spoke Kate realized with a great surge of affection why this marriage had so triumphantly lasted for twenty-five years. "I hate to grant a principle for the other side," he said, "but you know I do find it amazing, helpful and affectionate American husband as I am, who married a woman because, among other attractions, she had brains and a mind of her own. I've been to tea—my dear, you've no idea how often I've been to tea; the poor chaps feel they should ask me home at least once, and no doubt dinner is an expense and horror—and, Kate, it is just as though these men have a perfectly behaved servant. We arrive, are greeted charmingly, the wife acting as if she were a geisha girl who'd outgrown the fascination originally required for the job, and then we are served tea. I mean actually served it, all sorts of cakes and sandwiches and whatnot she's spent hours concocting, and after we've stuffed ourselves and told her what a good tea it was, we simply leave, I saying thank you politely, and her husband, my colleague, giving her a peck and saying, in effect, expect me when you see me. I don't deny that when the women's movement was getting under way in the States, I used to dream about a docile little wife the center of whose life I was, but you know, I've discovered it's not only embarrassing, it's bad for the character. There's a woman who works in our laboratory, and I asked her about it; she's a very important and competent woman. 'Oh, well,' she said, as though I'd asked her why some Oxford men don't get involved with boats during Eights Week, 'most English women aren't interested in liberation.' She made it sound like backgammon, or higher thought— some new fad. And yet she's far more liberated herself, to use that frightful word, than any American woman I've met professionally. Does her job, glad to have it, and no nonsense."

"Hugh," Phyllis said, staring at him, "that's the longest speech you have ever made in my presence since the first fine, careless rapture; what's more, its the greatest tribute to the women's movement in America yet enunciated. I apologize for even considering the soccer game."

"I couldn't have helped you at a soccer game anyway, my dear. I'm not much at watching the lower classes cavort. My offer included only elegant Oxford events. I had in mind something like a pleasant afternoon on the Balliol cricket grounds. That offer is still open. Farewell, my dear ladies. I am glad, Kate, to have seen you at last."

"He always vanishes like that," Phyllis said when Hugh was gone.

"Well, this is how he described tea. Maybe every

woman should spend one year as the little wife at home. Be thankful you're lucky enough to have done it when it isn't a lifetime commitment. But I have to admit"—Kate laughed—"he did slip back into that sleek masculine world with indecent haste. Still, it has made him a feminist, let us not forget."

"Let us not. Tell me about Whitmore—the best soap opera ever."

"I hope her life wasn't that," Kate said.

"I only meant soap opera in the sense of being presented in daily installments. But I don't know why all this prejudice against soap opera anyway. It's only the feminine version of melodrama, and frequently much better. Anyway, the sense I've been getting from your Whitmore and friend Cecily and Frederica Tupe—fabulous name—is that, in the beginning anyway, before Tupe became Reston and Cecily became Ricardo, life was clearer for them than it would be now. Is that only an illusion of time?"

"I don't think it was so different then from now," Kate said. "I'm sure when Whitmore and Hutchins and Tupe went to live in London and support themselves on free-lancing and a little help from their families, there were as many raised eyebrows then as now. It seems clearer because they were unusual in knowing what they wanted. People who know what they want are always unusual, particularly if what they want isn't to be found along one of the well-worn paths furnished by society for the use of the young. Whitmore's school was bombarded during the war—shot at, I mean, by guns from ships. She not only discovered the excitement of all that, of being one of those left behind when fearful parents had removed their, in Whitmore's opinion, less fortunate daughters from the school on the coast; she learned that courage is not an exclusively male virtue. I mean courage under fire. Some young man from the nearby town, when the bombardment started, grabbed a horse and nearly ran over a lot of children getting away from the place, while the women at the school were calmly helping everyone. Later she had a brother killed in the war and knew that she had to meet his courage with hers, offer her life, really, to prove that his hadn't been offered in vain. That's why she joined the army, of course."

"What did Whitmore actually do in the war? Nursing?"

"No, she was really in the army—Queen Mary's Army Auxiliary Corps was its proper name. It was all very daring and new at that time, and she was a sergeant. Used to march the girls around, snapping out orders: 'Left march, eyes right'—great fun, I should think, for someone who'd never cared for being ladylike and who was built like a Valkyrie and looked like Athena."

"She didn't have a commission, and her from Somerville?"

"No. I don't think many women had commissions, except the nurses, who were terribly isolated, poor things; they weren't allowed to hobnob with the enlisted men and were forbidden to associate with the officers. When Whitmore finally ended up in France and in a signal unit, there was only one woman officer. They were telegraphists, repaired telephone lines, did clerking—that sort of thing. There was a male signal unit there with them. It was a heavily bombed area, so the two signal units—maybe they were really one; I'm very

151

weak on military matters—were hidden in the country-side and Whitmore used to ride about on horseback with some of the soldiers. Her letters are remarkable. Frankly, if I could imagine a male army corps of Americans, I'd assume they'd be raping any women they could get hold of, the way they always do in plays and movies, but there seems to have been an innocence about all this. The French, with their usual opinion of the English, suspected the worst, but, at least from Whitmore's accounts, they were wrong, everyone was just WAAC's and Tommies together. It was the end of a world, of course."

"And then she came back to Somerville?"

"Michaelmas term, 1919. And shared a railway coach with Tupe or Hutchins or maybe both. Anyway, they met. The next year they lived together in lodgings, not far from where you are now, I expect. Then they went down to London together and started to write and meet interesting people and enjoy the optimistic twenties. Tupe dwindled into wife, but the other two kept at it for a number of years. Then Hutchins married her Ricardo and came to America; she found the secret of solitude and art, but Whitmore? Whitmore just kept struggling with the two ideas that wouldn't let hold of her: women must cease thinking they were ordained by God to be servants, and she must increase her sense of her opportunity to live life. All her novels and poems were attempts to catch life, behind the everyday reality. The critics haven't noticed them, except the last, and that they ignored because it was popular. She made herself live to finish *North Country Wind*, there's lots of evidence of that. Well," Kate finished up lamely, "they're all dead now."

"But you know," Phyllis said, "the same class thing goes on. Hugh wasn't just trying to be funny with his new Oxford manner when he talked about the lower classes at soccer. He told me he asked in the SCR about one of the younger dons, and was told that his antecedents weren't especially refined."

"It's only just occurred to me," Kate said, "but I dare say most of the professional athletes in America don't exactly come from the upper reaches of society, but nobody bothers to mention it. Is England still as madly class conscious as ever, or is it just crustier dons Hugh meets in his line of work?"

"Not a bit. Some quiet young man in Hugh's laboratory came up to Oxford originally on a scholarship from a state school, and soon after he came up he attended a meeting of a socialist club; the first question someone standing about asked him was what public school he'd been at. He hasn't let off being angry yet, Hugh says, and he's had one academic success after another ever since."

eleven

Kate could not prolong her stay beyond the original two weeks, and May 22 was at hand. What with reading the letters at Somerville, interspersed with the Whitmore novels, all of which Somerville had, and on alternate days reading the Hutchins novels in the Bodleian—not to mention the talks and strolls with Phyllis —Kate would barely manage to finish up on schedule. She had to return in time for the last of Leo's baseball games. The St. Anthony crisis appeared to have achieved a quietus, at least for the present. Meanwhile, in Oxford, Kate found herself coming to alarming conclusions about Max. One evening she would argue them away as idiotic fancies, the next they would appear to her the height of rationality. She might have continued alternating between these two possibilities indefinitely had she not returned to the hotel one evening about nine-thirty to find a message asking her to call Mr. Reston.

Kate dialed the number provided, and found herself speaking to Merton College. "Mr. Reston, please," she asked, uncertain what, or how, or why Max was there. But when Mr. Reston came on the phone, it was not Max, but Herbert Reston.

"I hope I'm not calling back too late," Kate said.

"Not at all. I just arrived this morning and had a word with Hugh; he suggested we might like to meet. He suggested, further, that you seemed most entranced with the college gardens, so I thought perhaps you would like to meet with me in the garden here. I shall come by and pick you up."

"Quite unnecessary," Kate said. "I'll meet you at the lodge in a few minutes, if you aren't too tired for so late a conversation."

"Not a bit. I'm only sorry there isn't time to arrange something more civilized, but alas, I must be in London again tomorrow. I'm only here for the night. In a few minutes, then."

In England, of course, in what they call the summer term, it remains light until ten at night. One forgets, Kate thought, walking toward Carfax, how far north England is, kept temperate by that marvelous phenomenon the Gulf Stream. Herbert Reston was there before her, waiting at the lodge, and the first thing Kate noticed about him was how little he resembled Max.

They walked together toward the garden, which overlooked Christ Church Meadow, and seemed to Kate everything lovely she had ever thought of in connection with England. "I haven't been invited to dine in hall," she said to Herbert Reston, "which is a minor ambition of mine, but I'm not sure this isn't lovelier, particularly since the college is closed to visitors."

"The garden *is* lovely, but I know what you are thinking, all the same: that I look nothing like Max. I'm friendly, bald, and roly-poly, while Max is tall, slim, and debonair. It has always been a trial to me."

"Max said you live in America."

"I spend much time in America, and much time here. Medical science, these days, is an international pursuit, I'm glad to say. Shall we sit down?"

"Forgive me," Kate said, dropping into a seat in her best ladylike manner so that he, too, might sit. "My thoughts have been wandering. You are kind to find a moment for me."

"You are a woman who has managed over the years to make a most marvelous impression on Hugh, which is singular indeed. He's not given to being impressed, one way or the other, as a rule. A failing, I fear, of the scientific mind when confronted with a personality rather than a theorem. Max has complained of it often."

"Were you good friends when you were boys?"

If Reston found the question odd, he did not show it. "Oh, yes, before we went off to school, naturally, and even at our prep school, where we were Reston major and minor, though from the first, major was so much smaller than minor, a fact I, major, had long since learned to live with. Max resembles our father, who was tall and thin, I our mother, who was small and, in later years, on the tubby side. Perhaps she would always have been plump, but doubtless young ladies know how to control these tendencies. Now that I think of it, my sister resembles me rather than Max, but she isn't nearly as tubby even today. One of my early memories of Max, actually, is when we were moved out of the night nursery to make room for my sister, and Max said, 'I don't so much mind sharing a room with Bertie, so long as I'm allowed to read after he's snoring.' Max was an infant at the time and couldn't read at all; we all thought he was frightfully stuck up, and from what people tell me, he still is. Not that I wasn't fond of him then as now."

"Max probably wouldn't be noticed at Oxford, but he does rather stand out in America. Haven't you seen him lately?"

"Since I do the major part of my work in Chicago, and Max didn't come to our nephew's wedding, I haven't seen him all that recently. Max dislikes weddings. He always sends a lavish gift and is thus not only forgiven but encouraged in his bad manners."

"So he explained to me. Mr. Reston, I'm afraid this will seem to you to be a very odd conversation, but as you say you leave tomorrow . . . I've become fascinated with your mother's two friends from Somerville, Dorothy Whitmore and Cecily Hutchins. Perhaps Hugh has told you. Would you tell me something about your mother? She's rather vague, somehow, compared to the other two. Oh, dear, I do hope that doesn't sound rude. Of course, I've never met any of them, and the letters of the other two are only at Somerville because of her kindness."

"Don't apologize. I think the years at Oxford and those few years in London were the happiest of my mother's life. It was not long after the war, you know, and my father swept her off her feet. I don't think it occurred to her to wonder what she would be doing twenty years hence. By then, Aunt Dorothy was dead— we always called her that—and Cecily Hutchins was in America writing novels. Oh, she enjoyed us children when we were young, I think, and she and my father lived a very gay life; one did, it seems, in the twenties. I remember in 1938 or so Aunt Dorothy's posthumous novel being made into a film, and Max and I were given

157

leave from school to come down to London to see the opening. Mother arranged about the scholarships left to Somerville by Dorothy's will." Reston sighed. "When one's an adolescent one doesn't really talk to one's parents, though I think Max talked a bit more, but I did have the sense that she came alive rather just after Dorothy's death, when there was the literary estate to be administered. Dorothy left Max first editions of all her novels, and she left me money toward a motorbike. I remember being faintly offended, though of course, I was pining for a motorbike. I also knew I ought to have been sorrier about her death than I was. Adolescents are such egocentric beasts. Now I wish I'd got to know her better."

"Did she visit you often?"

"She did. We saw her rather a lot after Cecily Hutchins left for America. But somehow it was always Max she talked to. Also, the two of them liked horses, which I never did. I used to bounce about in the saddle, and the first chance the horse had it would always bounce me off. Max, you know, was born grown up, like his namesake, Beerbohm."

"Was he named after Beerbohm?"

"Oh, I always suspected so, but my mother denied it. She said it was an old family name, but I never found it anywhere. Aunt Dorothy thought it was perfect."

The evening had closed in. Through the tall trees Kate could still see the sky, light against their dark branches, but day was over. "Do you remember," she asked, "when Max was born? Remember exactly, I mean?"

"Not a bit. Children weren't invited to consider the facts of life, not even in the twenties. I was four and shipped off to stay with Grandmama at the sea. When I returned there he was, established in Nanny's arms and looking as though he owned the place. Max managed to look like that even at the age of several weeks. I remember Nanny showing Max off to visitors and saying, 'You wouldn't believe it, it's that fair.' By the time my sister came along three years later, I thought the whole process a frightful bore. By then, of course, I knew where babies came from. When I asked my mother about Max, she said she'd found him under a gooseberry bush in the garden. Like most children, I managed not to make the mistakes my parents made with me when I became a father, even if I made every other one in the book; my children knew where babies came from even when they were so young they couldn't have cared less. Life is odd, isn't it?"

"Very odd," Kate said, "and you're kind as can be to talk to me. Do you find Oxford much changed from one visit to the next?"

"Oh, yes, Oxford changes. That's another way Max and I are different. He doesn't like change, while I at least admit it's inevitable, if not always in exactly the form we would choose. But I must say, you in hall would be most welcome. I hope to see it someday."

They began to walk back toward the gate. "Are you staying in England long?" Kate asked.

"Back to Chicago for me, alas, since it's beastly hot there right now. But I do hope we can meet again, Miss Fansler. You've made me think of my long-lost youth, and that hasn't happened in dog's years."

"You've been kindness itself answering one impertinent question after another. Do you think your mother would have liked to be a scholar?"

"Heavens, no. She was brought up bilingual, and took her degree in French. She used to read madly through everything, and take in all the ideas without getting a fact straight. She wasn't a scholar like the other two. They might have stayed at Oxford with fellowships if they hadn't decided to go off to London to live on nothing and write and work for the League of Nations. It was Mother's good luck they did decide to go, because otherwise she'd have lost them sooner. Good night, Miss Fansler; better still, au revoir."

Kate said good night, and wandered off deep in thought.

She was at Somerville so early the next morning that she had to loiter under the beeches waiting for the librarian to open up. She determined to seek in the papers, particularly in the letters, the evidence she was by now fairly certain would be there. It was not simple marital devotion which made her, pacing the path, think of Reed. She could hear him already warning her against leaping to a conclusion. But she wasn't leaping; she was approaching a conclusion with all the deliberation of a dog stalking a woodchuck. "Not theorizing ahead of your data, are you, Kate, as they say in the literature?" She could hear his voice as though he stood beside her. "Certainly not," she answered, startling the librarian, who came rushing up with a tale about a stalled bus and an impertinent bus driver. The librarian lived in North Oxford.

Once safely hidden in a bay with the papers, Kate looked particularly at the war years. There had been a male unit of the signal corps in France. Whitmore's letters home reported riding with a sergeant, who shared her passion for horses, on work horses borrowed from the French farms nearby. There might have been a man from before the war. But it was likely that anyone she would have met or loved at home would have been acceptable to her family, and Kate, hot in pursuit of a theory, was seeking a lower-class lover.

The question was, where had Whitmore met him? If she had really been, as she seemed, of a leftist turn of mind, she might have met him in a socialist club somewhere. But that was the sort of thing likelier to occur in the thirties, certainly. Kate, who could have told you exactly what sort of church group would have met in what town and why in Victorian England, was uncomfortably vague about the social life in the twenties outside of London literary circles. Anything, of course, was possible, but Kate inclined toward the theory of the wartime lover. Perhaps he turned up again in London after being demobilized and taking a series of unsatisfactory jobs. He might, after all, have worked at anything. The point was, the point had to be, that he had returned to Whitmore in London and become her lover. Why didn't they marry? Perhaps marriage didn't suit her; perhaps the man was married already, and this was only the drunken reliving of a wartime romance. Perhaps she was one of those independent types who wanted a baby and didn't want a husband, and took care the father shouldn't know who he was, or that he was. Questions of paternity had an odd effect on one's pronouns.

The London years when the three were there together were, unfortunately, the least documented. Seeing each other regularly, they had little reason to write, and their letters to their families (at least Whitmore's) were by

161

now of the perfunctory rather than the confessional sort. Wait a minute, there ought to be some dates here. Kate went to consult *Who's Who*. Max had been born in 1926, his brother Herbert in 1922, the same year (though at the other end) as his parents' marriage.

Cecily had moved to America with Ricardo in 1925. Therefore, if there was any discussion of the whole matter between the three of them, some at least of those letters ought to have been with Cecily's papers and ought, at this very moment, to be sitting safely in the Wallingford. Kate could not be certain, but she was willing to wager a considerable sum that they were not at the Wallingford or, perhaps, anywhere else.

Hold on a minute, Kate said to herself; hold on. Are you going to expound this highly libelous theory to anyone? Once in anyone's head, the idea will be very hard to get out, and there isn't a particle of evidence. Well, wasn't there? The whole story was so straightforward Kate, indeed, had to prevent herself trying it out on the librarian. But one must remember this was not a literary exercise of the sort that used to be undertaken, with such enthusiasm, in a search for the parentage of Shakespeare or Prince Albert, or that was still undertaken in an attempt to establish the authorship of Héloïse's letters to Abélard. The ramifications of this particular little problem were legal, and brutish, and nasty, and Gerry Marston's family might have something to say about it, not to mention the law and the courts. Go slow, Kate. Can you find one shred of evidence?

She thought, as her mind dashed about after phantoms, of the letter from Leo about the soccer game, and the discussion with Phyllis and Hugh that had followed. Hugh had talked of: the lower classes. A phrase, after all, with a meaning in England it simply would not have in America. One might speak of hard-hats, or blue-collar workers, or domestic servants, but apart from snobs and fools, no one minded who one's parents had been. But in England, where one mentioned antecedents, where the lower classes wore different hats and talked differently, whether or not you'd been to a public school changed your life. Kate recalled having read in an English paper that boys were chosen at the age of twelve as likely prospects for professional soccer, and trained for that career, frankly and openly. Professional football teams in America were not even allowed, legally, to approach a boy in college. Would someone with Max's taste and Max's conservative turn of mind want to trade in a father who was the younger son of the younger son of a duke for a working-class member of the armed forces and a feminist girl whose morals were no better than they should be?

Again Kate drew herself up. What about a will? Had Whitmore made a will? Of course she had; the librarian had told Kate all about it on the first day. Those were the scholarships at Somerville Herbert Reston had referred to. Dorothy Whitmore had left the royalties from her books toward a scholarship fund for a girl who had had to work before she came to Oxford. Here fate had played a beautiful trick, for the posthumous novel had been so successful, *and* sold to the films; the scholarship fund now paid the way for five or more girls every year. But surely it was important that the money was for girls who had to work. There *was* a sympathy for the working classes that nothing could argue away. No doubt Frederica had offered to adopt

Max, had already adopted him, had said: There is no need for you to leave him any money. How much money, in any case, did Whitmore have? Could anyone have guessed that *North Country Wind* would be a best seller and made into a successful movie? Going to the window to look out on the tennis lawn and the flower beds beyond, Kate thought suddenly of Graves wandering around Somerville in his pajamas and dressing gown, being saluted by the man who would become his moral tutor because he, Graves, was an officer. "Social life was dislocated," Crackthorne had written. Yes, indeed; it had to have been the war.

She had to try this out on someone. She would lay the whole business before Phyllis. Phyllis had a sharply clear mind and a forthright manner. If Kate was pursuing chimeras, Phyllis, bless her, would be the first to say so.

twelve

Phyllis said so, loudly, clearly, in no uncertain terms, when she had heard Kate through to the end of what she called the most preposterous story since Ian Fleming's unfortunate demise. "You're wandering, dear," she announced, not unkindly.

Kate found her attitude a relief, in a way. It really had been looking all too clear-cut and obvious, which nothing in life ever is.

"Put your objections to one side a moment, nonetheless," she said, "and listen to two more aspects of the problem. One of these is Max's writing and public image; the other is the personality of the young woman who was Dorothy Whitmore. As to Max. I copied down out of *Who's Who* a list of his publications. The titles, and the books themselves, if it comes to that—I've read most of them; he's a friend, God help me—are all aimed at setting right the inevitable decline from proper standards, whether in art or daily life, usually both. About daily life he's not quite so outspoken in print, if you'll forgive the phrase. But at a time, I can assure you, when most faculty and administration were, if not exactly happy about student revolutions, and so on, at least aware that some dislocation of power had

165

taken place in our society, Max was being his old authoritarian self, with an extraordinary blindness to the realities of the Vietnam war. All right, nod away, you agree and I ought to make my point, if any. My point is: here is the last man who wants to set forth into the maelstrom of rediscovered feminist writers and women's studies the story of his birth to a woman who resembles all too closely the radicals he loathes today and, far worse, his having been fathered not by some tall, beautifully arrogant creature who resembled, from all I can gather, Lord Riddlesdale in the Sargent portrait, but a lower-class out-of-job nobody without a spot of culture or breeding."

"All right, I take your point, I really do, believe me, Kate. When you're discussing Max's horror at everything from the modern world to the discovery of this terrible secret, all set down among Cecily's papers up in Maine for anyone to read, yes, I follow you, and even pant enthusiastically behind. But face what you're saying. That he discovered that Marston child, that student of yours, in among the papers, enticed her out to the rocks, and murdered her. All to keep the story of his shameful birth from the world. Too nineteenth-century, dear, not to say eighteenth. And it isn't as though some marvelous inheritance stood in the balance. If there was anything to inherit, and we don't know that there was, you can be sure with a family like the Restons that it went, firmly entailed, to the oldest son, who was not Max. I've always disapproved of primogeniture, by the way, since the only possible attitude toward one's children is share and share alike, but one does have to admit that if it's not good for the children, it's great for

166

the property, which stays in one piece through the generations."

"And sends the younger sons out to marry with the newly rich middle classes and enrich not only their pockets but their gene bank."

"No doubt. But the point is that there is no question of inheritance here. I realize that Max is a snob, perhaps the original and authentic snob, after which they threw away the mold, but I can't see him killing anyone to preserve his reputation for impeccable birth. And," she finished up, with a certain air of having exhausted the subject, "all Max had to do was destroy the papers, or waft them out of sight. It would be his word against the girl's, guilty of breaking and entering anyway, and who would listen to *her*? Will you have beer or Scotch?"

"Beer," Kate said. "I've become addicted, as you said I would. Perhaps you are right," she added, reverting to Max. "But I don't think you are. I shall have to consider a course of action. What do you suppose the papers consisted in?"

"What papers? The papers that don't exist, except in your girlish imagination?" She handed Kate a beer.

"There must have been letters," said Kate, accepting the beer and ignoring the comment. "Letters from Whitmore to Frederica, which were sent to Cecily at Whitmore's death."

"If Whitmore was such a bloody socialist, flinging herself into the arms of a workingman, like Helen into the arms of Leonard Bast, out of sheer pity, why on earth did she call him Max? The last name on earth for a lower-class love child."

"Precisely. Frederica's choice, I have no doubt. To distract attention from his origins. Phyllis, think! How

167

many brothers do you know who resemble each other as little as Max and Herbert Reston? One short, one tall, one fat, one thin—all that is possible, but there's always *some* resemblance. My brothers have each grown middle-aged in his own gruesome way, but once you know they're brothers, there's no discounting the resemblance. Even I can be seen to look a bit like them, in the dusk with a lamp behind me."

"Have you ever wondered who your father was, you late child, you? Of course, the difference is, if your father turned out to be a sheet-metal worker from Skaneateles and your mother someone who had chained herself to the White House in the Hoover administration, you'd be gladder than glad."

"People didn't chain themselves to the White House in the Hoover administration; they camped along the Potomac."

"You haven't even seen Max and Herbert together."

"They feel different, if you take my meaning."

"So do you and your brothers. Kate, Kate, what is to be the end of all this?"

"You didn't know Gerry Marston. She was a lovable child. *Her* parents were sheet-metal workers, or as near as makes no matter. And she would have made a name for herself—would, at any rate, have had the joy of writing a biography, which *is* a great joy, in its perverse way. The only person Max ought to write a biography of is Metternich. Or Talleyrand."

"Suggestion. From Phyllis to Kate, for the use of. Read all you can on this and shut, otherwise, up. When you get back to New York, you can tell Reed all about it or even, if absolutely necessary, Max. But do tell him in a crowded dining room somewhere, not on some rocks in Maine. And don't drink anything that smells or tastes peculiar."

"I don't believe," Kate said, "that you're half as skeptical as you make out. But it's good advice, and I shall take it."

"That's a wonder," Phyllis said.

Kate had some mail, just at the end of her visit.

Reed wrote a note to say there had been fascinating developments in the St. Anthony's bit; Finlay and Ricardo had finally gone to the headmaster and admitted the whole thing. The faculty insisted that the headmaster write to Harvard with the facts, or what continued to be called the alleged facts. Leo and his friends were being talked about in a way that Reed thought rather worried Leo, but that Leo would probably survive. Reed said that he thought all would be looking up from now on for Leo, and that he, Reed, would be rather glad when she came home.

Mr. Sparrow wrote from the library of the Wallingford about his new exhibition, and how well Max Reston was doing with the papers. He added his regret that Kate, being a woman, would miss the inside of All Souls.

Phyllis and Hugh made plans for a continental tour, after which they would return, in the fall, to the States. It was clear that Phyllis was so eager to get back into harness that she contemplated even the wonders of Greece, which she had always longed to see, with a lackluster eye.

At the end of her two weeks, then, Kate hired a car to drive her to Heathrow, and found herself upon a 747 headed home. She had, in the compartment above

169

her head, a particularly beautiful sweater for Reed, an old brass hunting horn for Leo, which required much breath to blow, and notes on all the Whitmore papers.

She also had by now a theory which no amount of caution could convince her was not, in its essence, true. Max had committed murder to hide the shame of his birth, and what in the world was she to do about it?

thirteen

In the end Kate made a clean breast of the whole thing
to Reed. After a bare twenty-four hours of catching up
on letters and messages, Kate abandoned the lot and
fled with Reed to the cabin in the Berkshires. The
meadow had grown lavishly since she had seen it in the
early spring, and the wind, when it blew, sent waves
through the tall grass as though it were the sea. Kate
had not realized how tired she had become, how constantly she had been responding to the young women
of the Oxford of long ago, nor how relentlessly she had
walked or bicycled the streets of Oxford, always in
search of some thought or memory or the ever renew-
able shock of joy when one comes yet again upon a
beautiful garden like that at New College. There was
indescribable relief in the fact that no one had taken
care of anything here in the Berkshires, that bushes and
trees grew and competed, nature red in tooth and claw,
if such can be said of the vegetable kingdom. "More
like the jungle of New Guinea," Reed had offered, as
they moved lazily from outside to in, from one collapsed chair to another, and allowed tired metaphors to
chase each other in their minds. Reed, too, had been
under pressure, and it was as though, Kate remarked,

someone had pulled the plug in the soles of their feet and let all the energy drain away.

Reed, whether because of the indolence of the life, or their remarkable closeness, or the tender, wandering, searching quality of their conversation—whatever the reason, he listened to the theory about Max without his usual acerbic response to Kate's high-flown speculations.

"You've found the one thing we never come across in actual criminal cases," he remarked. "A subtle motive. Worthy of all you literary types. And *very* nineteenth-century, protecting the story of one's humble origins. If his books are half as high and mighty and laying down the law of proper values as you suggest, I do suppose he'd do anything to whitewash the record of his meager beginnings. It's a triple blow: not only was he adopted, which is not so terrible a thought in this day and age, not only does he know he was illegitimate, which has ceased to be a legal and mostly social blight; he actually knows who Mama and Papa were, or at least the sort they were, and he doesn't like it a bit. That is, if the letters suggest what you so happily assume they do."

"And what to do, Reed?"

"There is only one thing to do, my darling Kate. Forget about it all. We couldn't prove a thing, not possibly. Oh, no doubt with ardent and systematic questioning we might establish that he was in Maine and not in the classroom in New York as he has claimed and we have too lightly accepted. Perhaps, pursuing with equal ardor investigations in Maine, we might find someone who saw him at what is called the operative moment. It wouldn't hold up before a grand jury for a moment, let alone in court. You'd never get an indictment. And you'd ruin a perfectly good career, incidentally."

"I was thinking of blackmail," Kate said.

"Were you indeed? There is no morality left anywhere in the world. I remember when that was the worst crime on the books, the most reprehensible, morally speaking. Fictional detectives refused to pursue blackmailers, saying, with a wave of their elegant hands, 'Let justice be done; I will not interfere.' "

"Let's call it judicious blackmail."

"Let's call it crime and forget about it."

"How can I forget about it, Reed? I know it's old-fashioned and sentimental and altogether not 'today' to talk of restitution, or making it up to Gerry Marston, or anything like that. But I did say to Leo, we both did, that one should do what one could. Not that I have to tell anyone anything. One can also be honorable by oneself, in secret."

"Only if one is God, or thinks one is."

"I don't believe that." Kate watched as a cardinal flashed across from tree to bush, his brightness making him more of a gift, somehow, than the birds of less glorious color. Yet he seemed unaware of it, and treated his duller-colored mate with a gallantry that would have done justice to Max. "If one begins something, one must carry it through. One simply does what one has to do at the time. 'I think that must have been what Krishna meant.' No, I'm becoming gaga in my middle years. You are right, you are absolutely right. We will forget the whole thing. I only wish, in a way, that you had seen her body, and known her."

"All right," Reed said as he took her in his arms.

173

"Max has found his way here before. Let him find it again. We'll drive into town after a while and make a telephone call."

In the end, it was quite late that night before they drove in and spoke to Max.

Their invitation had been brief and unadorned with explanation, but he had accepted. The next day Max, the only visitor known to the cabin, once again made his way across the uncut meadow. This time he did not pause to search for a path. He had, Kate thought, understood and accepted all the conditions this time.

They sat around the table, Kate and Reed having decided that this was, on the whole, the best place for their conversation. They might have sprawled outside on the uncut grass, but apart from the difficulty of imagining Max sprawling, a slightly more formal and even enclosed ambiance seemed called for. Since there were only two straight chairs, Kate and Max sat facing each other across the table, and between them Reed balanced on the window sill, fiddling with his pipe and making his presence somehow indefinite, as though he might, if called upon, emerge from his state of abstraction, but he rather hoped not.

"You probably wonder why we've asked you to come," Kate weakly began. She was hoping, by this tender lead, to get Max talking, to make him begin and spill it all out so that she, finally, could say, 'Well, what are we going to do about it?' and get down to issues. But Max was far too experienced a duelist for that. Kate had long since discovered that the majority of humanity, of whatever age and degree of education or position, would, given half a chance, talk on about themselves with little or no prodding. But Max had an orderly mind, a disciplined personality, and not even middle age had trapped him into the need for self-revelation. He responded to Kate's idiotic sally only with a nod, and she was forced to begin again. She was careful not to catch Reed's eye.

"I've been at Oxford for two weeks," she said. "Most of Dorothy Whitmore's papers are at Somerville, where your mother beqeathed them. But the letters that Whitmore wrote to Cecily Hutchins after she came to America remained, of course, in the house in Maine. I rather expected," she lamely concluded, "that they would be among the Hutchins papers at the Wallingford."

"No doubt Cecily destroyed them," Max said. "Isn't that what you would have done in her place?"

"No," Kate said. "Not if I had determined to keep the lot for posterity. Cecily was far too intelligent, that's obvious, to have been one of those people like Swinburne's sister, who print all the innocuous parts of the letters and burn the rest. I think those letters were there, Max, and what's more, I think you know it. What's furthermore," she said, trying without success to keep all emotion from her voice, "is that you destroyed them."

"Perhaps that is why Cecily made me her literary executor, so that I would destroy what I judged best destroyed."

"That isn't what you said on the way to Maine, or in New York either. You said the point was to protect the materials from exploitation, but also, there was the implication, from destruction. You were more qualified because more literary and scholarly than her children."

"I agree. It was foolish of me to suggest otherwise. Besides, as an art historian I have a profound sense of the importance of preserving materials. Destroying evidence is counter to everything I believe in, even in times of discretion, like this one. Forgive me for being unable to resist parrying with you. What are you suggesting, Kate?"

"I'm suggesting," Kate began, feeling that control of the conversation had passed to Max, and she could not seem to regain mastery of it. But after all, she told herself, I hold the cards. He's bluffing. He's trying to find out what's in my hand. "I'm suggesting that those letters existed, that, somehow, Gerry Marston found them, and that . . . that you were forced to recover them from her."

Max leaned across the table as though the point of an anecdote had at last been achieved, and he didn't wish to miss the punch line.

"And what," he asked, reaching his hand, palm up, across the table almost in a gesture of supplication, "was in the letters Miss Geraldine Marston found?"

"I know what was in them, Max."

"Do you, Kate? Tell me."

"The truth about your less than perfectly refined antecedents," she said, getting up and beginning to walk about the cabin. "The fact that your father was not the younger son of the younger son of a duke, but a noncommissioned nobody whom Whitmore had met in the war in France and gone on to love, or perhaps only to pity, in London, and you were the result. All the letters must have discussed what would become of you, what Whitmore would do. There may even have been letters later, when Whitmore knew she was dying,

176

about whether she would recognize you in her will. In the end, of course, she didn't. You had an identity and an inheritance. You were a Reston, absolutely, the younger son of a younger son of a younger son."

She turned then to look at Max and saw that Reed's eyes were on him also. He sat back in his chair, perfectly still, as though objectively considering the likelihood of his having done murder. One could almost hear the fine mind working, the possibilities being weighed. He crossed one elegantly shod leg over the other and removed a cigarette case from inside his jacket; he made quite a business of lighting the cigarette and returning the case and lighter to his pocket. "I take it I need not ask permission to smoke," he said, "since Reed has anticipated me. Would you care for a cigarette?" he asked Kate, again reaching for his case.

"No, thank you," Kate said. "I've sworn off, more's the pity." She hadn't. She didn't, she realized with astonishment, want to smoke one of Max's cigarettes from that perfect case. There is such a thing as being too civilized. I would even be grateful, Kate thought, if his socks were in puddles around his ankles.

"Tell me more about my parents," he said. "Do, Kate. You can hardly ask me to discuss such a matter unless you are willing to tell me what you know. They may have hung dukes with a silken rope, but they didn't ask them to weave it themselves."

So once again Kate told the story. "I realize it is all supposition," she added when she had finished. "But I think it is also capable of proof; I'm willing to try."

"And there is, I assume, a price for your not trying. Forgive me for putting it so crudely."

"Not at all. It's a crude business. Damn crude. And

177

part of the price," she harshly said, "is to tell me what happened."

"Ah, I was afraid of that. I didn't kill her, you know. I'd heard from the old lady on the road, who was a friend of Cecily's, that she'd seen the girl about. She didn't get particularly close, and didn't know it was a girl. That's the result of your marvelous unisex world," he added, "with no taste left in dressing and everyone in trousers." It was the first return of his old supercilious manner. But he soon dropped back into a steady tone. "I flew to Boston one day after my class, and from Boston to a small airport near Cecily's village. My supposed horror of flying has been exaggerated—by me. All done with cash and no need for names, or not real names. When I got there I took a taxi to town and hired a horse. It was past the tourist season, and they were glad enough to rent one for cash down. I always knew how to ride, and I had changed my clothes to those of a roughneck so that I might escape notice in, so to speak, my proper being. On a horse it was easy enough to investigate the roads until I found the right one. I asked directions only once or twice, of children returning from school. Even if they remembered the occasion, or if someone asked them, all they could have described was a man on horseback in work clothes and a cap.

"Your Miss Marston was there when I arrived. Inside the house. She may have been a lovely student, my dear, but she was a housebreaker and a thief. God knows how long she'd been there. She'd found the important papers, all right, thanks to Cecily's orderly file cabinets. You didn't need an ABD or even a Ph.D. to find anything in Cecily's file cabinets.

178

"Picture it for yourself. She had discovered what no one must ever know. Only *she* knew it, so far. Even if I managed to refuse her publication of the papers, that knowledge would spread from her into the wide world; such knowledge always does. Of course, I didn't appear upset to her. I asked her what she thought we should do about it. In the end we agreed to walk about the place and talk it over. I put before her the criminal aspects of her behavior, and she promised that she would mention the matter to no one. Promises are easy, but I have learned that only those trained in a stable culture know the value of a word, and of trust. I couldn't think what to do, if you want to know. And then we came to the sea, and below us were the rocks. I suggested we climb on them—it's very tempting, as you yourself demonstrated that day in Maine."

"Yes," Kate said, "I've appreciated that. You suggested seeing the rocks, but I begged to clamber about on them, all by myself. You didn't even have to suggest it."

"Don't be bitter, my dear. It shows something wonderful about your spirit, and Miss Marston's—though yours, I trust, would not lead to housebreaking and the reading of other people's mail, at least outside of libraries. She slipped on the rock; she was wearing some quite unsuitable shoes, despite the trousers, and didn't realize what rocks are like, or the seaweed between. She slipped and hit her head; she fell face down into one of the pools. Even then I wasn't a murderer. I tried to raise her. But she was no mean weight, and I couldn't get a foothold. In the end, I left her where she lay."

"And contrived to lead me there, like an idiot child,

to find the body and recognize her. It is loathsome to be manipulated."

"That is not true. I did quite simply want your company on that trip. But you will never believe that. And now, I suppose, this is all to come out. All about the letters."

"Not," Kate said, "if I can have the letters."

"I see. I'm to give you the blackmail weapons into your hands, and you promise not to use them."

"Exactly. Surely my antecedents are refined enough for you to believe that."

"I deserved that comment and bow before it. And what will you do with the letters when you get them?"

"Add them to the Wallingford collection, sealed until some future date. No one will know your terrible secret until their knowing can no longer matter to you."

"And to how many people have you told this story?"

"Only two. Reed, whose discretion you can and will have to rely on, and a woman friend whom I trust and whom you will have to trust also."

"I see. You didn't, I'm to gather, confront brother Herbert with it?"

"No, Max, I've been decent. My questions to Herbert were not exactly palpitating with propriety, but he certainly had no idea what I was after; I'm sure he put it all down to a rather heated and American interest in English cultural history. Probably he's been in America long enough to know that most Americans ask personal questions as a matter of course."

She returned to the table and sat down again in her chair. "You know, Max, I made a trip to London especially to visit the Tate and look at Whitmore's portrait, which I first saw that day in Maine. She was

180

like a goddess, blond and strong and courageous. Fair, like you."

"Really, my dear; my father—that is, Reston—was fair also. The English run to fairness, you may have noticed."

"How often you must have seen that portrait, Max, when you visited Cecily as a boy from England, and in all the visits after. Did it never occur to you to be proud of her as a mother?"

"Never. Even had I known she was my mother, which, you must remember, I didn't. Not till I saw those letters that day with your Miss Marston did I know. I never even suspected. And if I had, I would have banished the thought as absolutely as possible. Who would want for a mother, however goddesslike, a feminist, a freethinker, a socialist, and a pacifist? It's everything I loathe. Nor am I reconstructed when it comes to women. I like them to be ladies, wives, and mothers, or at worst, eccentric and appealing old maids. If they write novels, as Cecily did, they should do it when their womanly duties have been fulfilled. It is better still if they do not write novels, as my mother, the woman I think of as my mother, did not. She merely spoke exquisite French and made her husband and children marvelously happy."

"It must have been a shock," Kate said, playing for time. She looked up at Reed, but he evidently did not consider she was in need of rescue. He continued in his role of silent witness.

"No more than this is," Max said. "All right, Kate. You hold all the cards. Suppose I promise you those letters in a few weeks—they've been put away, and I simply can't get off to fetch them much sooner, though

I will try—and leave them to be preserved and sealed off by you. Have I your word and Reed's, that no more will be heard of all this, ever again, no matter what turns up?"

"Why should it be I who give my word? I hold the cards, remember?"

"Because I am here, instead of receiving a visit from the District Attorney's office. Or would it be from the office of the chief investigator of Maine, whatever his title? Need we take it all one step at a time? You want the letters for posterity, though I don't think this is a necessary way to get them. I want to know I will never be accused of murder. Is there some more complicated way to put it?"

"Well," Kate said, aware that she had not made a very good showing from beginning to end in this confrontation, "let's leave it at that, then. I'll arrange with Mr. Sparrow to deposit with him the sealed letters. Nor shall I approach you again for further payments. Mine is a one-time blackmail only."

"No doubt many blackmailers have said that."

"No doubt. But I am unique. You will have to believe that, if you are to believe anything."

"So you are, Kate. So you are. You have my word the letters will be in your hands in a day or two. I have yours that they will be in no one else's while I live."

"Agreed," Kate said. But she did not accept his proffered hand. Slowly he withdrew it, flushing, and walked out, across the uncut meadow to his waiting car and chauffeur.

"And what," Kate said to Reed, "will he do now? Suppose he just destroys the letters and denies the whole thing? What's become of my evidence?"

"No chance of that, unless he decides discussions of murder and his bastardy are worth it. Since his motives are, you conclude, to prevent the truth from coming out while he is still alive to face up to it, he will not want you there to spread it abroad together with accusations of homicide."

"Reed. You're not suggesting he's going to kill himself?"

"I doubt it. But in this game you're playing, my love, isn't the culprit always left alone in the library with someone's old army revolver?"

"Reed, you don't like Max. I never realized that."

"Neither did I. No, I don't like him at all, now that you mention it. Look, it's no good suggesting we don't think of him, but let's at least not talk of him. Can we manage that?"

"We just might," Kate said.

part four

{ June }

fourteen

Almost eight days had passed since the meeting in the cabin, and Kate began to think that Max had funked it. Oddly enough, though she knew him to be capable of some of the highest crimes in the book, she did not think he would break his word or renege on an agreement, any more than he would have been capable of destroying papers of historical value. Honor among thieves, I suppose, she thought, but nonetheless, she searched the obituary section of the paper and answered the telephone a bit more readily, more anxiously than had been her wont.

And then on the first night of June he telephoned to ask if he might come for a brandy. Kate, receiving a nod across the room from Reed, said they would be glad to see him.

When he turned up, as mannered, as dapper, as in control of himself as ever, Kate realized she had been battling chimeras.

"My apologies for having been so long. I was detained by service to another and hope, therefore, to be forgiven. One ought not to offer one's services and then use that as an excuse for failing in one's other obligations, but—the fact is, I have been helping

Randolph Brazen with his book. He is old and needs some intelligent help, but the book will be important; I'm sure of that. I told him I was to be late for an appointment, and he insisted on writing you a note."

Randolph Brazen had been the most famous columnist of his day, in a day when political columnists were the pundits of the earth. Kate could remember his name being uttered by her elders much as the name of the Delphic oracle must have been spoken earlier. "I didn't know he was still living," she admitted, accepting the note from Max. She read it aloud. " 'To those who have a proper claim upon Max's time, forgive me for having kept him beyond his allotted stay. His usefulness to me, and his kindness, have been great indeed; I would consider it a personal favor if you would forgive him his tardiness, for which I am wholly responsible.' Where does he live?" Kate asked.

"In Wilton, Connecticut, in a lovely old house. All his papers are there. Reading over some of his columns of forty years ago, one realizes what a loss the lack of such a man is to us today. He had that now downgraded quality common sense." Max let this remark drop into the silence. Then he went to the hall to fetch a cardboard envelope—it was like Max not to carry anything so middle class as a briefcase—and removed a file folder from it. "The letters," he said. "All that Cecily had from Whitmore at the time. There were none from my mother, from Frederica, which means that either Cecily destroyed them or that she returned them to Frederica. From several things she said, I think that is most likely. My mother in her turn must have destroyed them, for they have never turned up. But the ones from Whitmore are evidence enough, if you want it."

"May I look at them?" Kate asked.

"I hope you will read them with care," Max said. "I should like your statement, to me at least, that the file seems sufficiently complete. No, don't take my word for it, though you have that. Read them."

"Later," Kate said. She opened the file and immediately recognized Whitmore's handwriting, of which she had seen so much at Somerville. It was an oddly childish hand, leaning sometimes one way, sometimes another, as though she had given up any attempt to be distinctive and was just getting her thoughts down. Kate had learned that the dons had complained about Whitmore's bad syntax and worse spelling, but by this date the illegibility of her writing had gone, perhaps because she was surer of what she was saying, and why. Kate placed the folder on the table.

"How about that brandy?" Reed asked.

"Thank you," Max said. He sat near Kate in silence, until the snifter was handed to him. "How nice; the proper way to drink fine brandy. One has the pleasure of the aroma first. To you, my dear."

"To Whitmore," Kate said; she drank Scotch and did not, at this moment, bother with the aroma. In fact, now she had permission, she desperately wanted to read the letters and could only with difficulty contain herself. It took all her social resources (which, Reed might have pointed out, were never extensive) to keep from glaring at Max as he nursed his brandy, swirling it lovingly in the large snifter and taking occasional tiny sips. She had the sense that Max knew what she was feeling, and that the knowledge in no way decreased his slow pleasure in his drink. He had actually taken to beginning a conversation on some political issue while warming the glass in his hands, and Kate had decided she would simply rise and plead the need of work, leaving Reed (who had, after all, brought him the brandy in that ridiculous glass) to cope, when Max suddenly drank off the rest and arose. He bowed slightly to Kate.

"Thank you, my dear, for your trust and your patience. I need hardly tell you how sad I am, and shall always be, about the accident to your student. Do believe, now that you know all the truth about me, that that fact also is the truth. May we meet again soon as though none of this had happened?"

"Soon, perhaps," Kate said. "Not right away."

"There is the whole summer to get through. But I look forward to inviting you to lunch in the fall. Please give me some reason to hope you will accept my invitation."

"Max, I hope to. Let's leave it at that."

"Good night, my dear. Good night, Reed."

Kate heard Reed walk with Max to the door, heard his good night and the door close.

"Do you want to read them?" Kate asked.

"No. Not unless there is something especially noteworthy. Somehow, the whole business makes me a trifle sick."

"I know. And yet I do so want to read them, Reed. Am I a beast? Yes, I am. But I feel Gerry Marston will not have died quite so idiotically if these will, at least, be read one day."

"If he saved them after her death, he would have

saved them in any case, and they would have been read one day. Never have I heard of a more stupid death."

Kate replaced the letters on the table. "You're right, of course."

"But not right to rob you of what is after all a perfectly legitimate pleasure, under the circumstances. I never can be less than frank with you, but not for a moment did I mean you ought not to read the letters." He left the room and Kate picked up the folder once again.

"The question is," Kate read in the middle of one of the letters in Whitmore's rather childish hand, "to what can one, should one, dedicate oneself? The dangers of self-pity and self-indulgence haunt me; yet I have a sense of destiny and, what is more, anger and defiance. I sometimes think men know nothing of life and have kept women shut up for so many centuries lest women discover this. Cecily, Cecily, I am ranting, but what an angel you are. I shall have the baby—that is determined, and please God, let it be a boy, with his destiny clear and sharp before him. Isn't it odd that none of us longs for daughters. You want to replace the neighbor boys murdered in the war, I expect, as I want to replace a brother. Frederica simply prefers males of any age. Except perhaps if women could be like *us*, you will quickly say. But how many like us are there? Frederica, at least, has given her husband a son already. Should he have loathed a daughter, do you think? I read somewhere that all parents, if they could choose the sex of their children, would want the first child to be a boy."

Kate suddenly felt herself back at Somerville. How like Whitmore to be going on about the sex of one's children, rather than, as one would have expected, their legitimacy. But turning several sheets, Kate came upon a letter dealing, she gathered, with this question. "No, Cecily, I shall not tell the father. Why ever should I? The choice was mine, the risk was mine, and the birth will be mine. He hasn't even troubled to enquire, and why should he? I scarcely encouraged him in a wild personal interest in me, or into thinking I had any great passion for him. It's all nonsense anyway, thinking you can make up to one man what you've robbed from another, or what the world has robbed him of. Because I cheated Gerald out of loving me, being too young and stupid to understand *his* passion, I try, like a fool, to make it up to this poor beast. Rosalind was right: men have died from time to time, and worms have eaten them, but not for love."

No, Kate thought, not for love, hardly ever for love. Always for hate, or pride, or vanity, or self-protection.

Whitmore's letters told Cecily, finally, of Frederica's offer to take over the baby as her own, "even if it is a girl." It was astonishing, really, with what bitterness Whitmore harped on this point. Frederica had pointed out that her freedom would not be imperiled as Whitmore's would, nor had she the possibility for a life of high accomplishment as Whitmore had. How could they know that Whitmore would be dead in ten years? Yet they had not been wrong. *North Country Wind* was one of those rare books, like *Middlemarch* and *Persuasion*, for which only a lifetime is adequate preparation. Within it—and this had played no small part in Kate's reconstruction of Max's parents—the heroine has a love affair with the town's most prominent male, a widower. This was profoundly shocking behavior in the village life pictured in the novel, but the reality of the passion had been evoked with skill: skill and knowledge.

Whitmore had died young. Frederica had found the most conventional and time-honored of fulfillments. Cecily had lived on to achieve what was clearly going to be great fame. Who knew? Perhaps Max's biography would bring Whitmore back into fame also, as Gerry Marston's study might have done.

There was nothing more for it but to deliver the letters, sealed, to the Wallingford. She must really put the story out of her mind. Once, in a lighter moment, Kate had remarked to Reed that her advice to Max had been similar to that of Lady Bracknell to Jack Worthing: "I would strongly advise you, Mr. Worthing, to make a definite effort to produce at any rate one parent, of either sex, before the season is quite over." With some persuasion, Max had produced the parent.

And thinking of parents, Kate reminded herself, if Max has found one real parent, Leo has adopted two substitutes. She had heard the door slam as Leo entered, never a silent process. Well, she thought, as he faced her, the letters in a packet at her side, however we have mucked it up, we have certainly done better than his real parents would have—not, alas, that that is saying much.

"What are you doing?" Leo asked. "You're usually bent over your desk at this hour."

"Whistling in the dark, that's what I'm doing. How are you?"

"It's all over," Leo said. "Anyhow, the main part. Harvard has said they can't come this year, they'll think about next, you know, consider them all over again then. Parents rushing around the school. Most of the faculty think the whole thing wasn't handled right, but I'm following Reed's advice and just smiling pleasantly and keeping a low profile. I only go in for classes."

"I know how you feel, or I think I do. You decide to do something, perform one small action, and suddenly it's a tide, the momentum is going, and there's no possibility of turning back. Somehow, even though you thought you foresaw all that would happen, you didn't know the pace would pick up so."

"You sound like you had the same experience."

"Not the same circumstances, but the same experience, I guess."

"The headmaster says now—not to me, of course, but everything gets around—that he would have acted immediately except that all the boys lied to him. Finlay and Ricardo, of course, they lied like I breathe, but also the ones he called in to ask if they'd seen Finlay at the exam. He says he acted properly—anyhow, that's what they say he says."

"I wouldn't think about that, if I were in your shoes. All he can feel, in that case, is grateful that it did get talked about, so that he wasn't compounding a felony, or countenancing a misdemeanor—Reed would know the phrase. And between you and me, Leo, phooey. He shouldn't be running the sort of school where any of these things happen, where students lie, where—oh, the hell with it. But don't expect him to be grateful; he won't be."

"Did you really say 'phooey' when you were young?"

"Leo, someday I'll tell you how old I was before I knew that damn wasn't the worst four-letter word available."

"Well, there's other news. We're playing an exhibition game against the next-best team on Sunday, June fourteenth. Money goes to the scholarship funds; in Central Park. Think you might come, or will you be up at the cabin?"

"Of course I'll come; I can leave early, if I'm there. What time is it?"

"Three. But don't feel you have to come. I just mentioned it because it's the last game of the season. The last game for St. Anthony's."

"And what a season it's been, athletically speaking, of course. I'll be there."

Leo ambled out to the kitchen in search of nourishment, and Kate thought that, oddly enough, both the problems were over together; the puzzles were solved. They were both very modern solutions, inconclusive and unsatisfactory, though in both her case and Leo's, to have done nothing would have been worse: satisfactory to the wrong people, and conclusive as to effect. Yet it was enough to make one long for the days of Victoria, when Tennyson would withhold his poem "Tithonus" from publication because, as one critic put it, "its world-weary pessimism was insufficiently tonic for the temper of the time." What could possibly be sufficiently tonic for the temper of this time?

fifteen

Alone in the cabin, Kate discovered that the solitude and the country had once again enabled her to collect herself. She had enjoyed what Mollie Panter-Downes, an English writer on whom Kate rather doted, called "the ultimate luxury of the well-off—the ability to avoid one's nearest and dearest at will."

Last night had been particularly clear, with the stars brilliant in the sky. Kate had known those who took comfort from the stars, as though the possible existence of other worlds minimized the sufferings of this one. Kate did not agree. Awed by spectacle, she nonetheless paid, with Whitman, her whole devotion to this world:

> The earth, that is sufficient,
> I do not want the constellations any nearer,
> I know they are very well where they are,
> I know they suffice for those who belong to them.

Trips to the moon, which Kate had watched on television, left her unmoved. The hoisting of the American flag on the moon she considered easily the worst example of bad taste since the Albert Memorial.

Three months ago Max had walked up the dirt road

and paused at the edge of her meadow, searching for a path. "Drive with me to Maine," he had said. Of course, Kate thought bitterly, I naturally took it for granted that my presence was desired for its own sake, that I was as ever the one to whom all thoughts turn. Is there any vanity greater than the vanity of those who believe themselves without it? But self-flagellation was not in order. Gerry Marston's death could not in any case have been prevented; no one else had suffered since. However monumental her own misconceptions, they had done harm to no one.

At least here, alone, she had been able to determine on a course of action, and must now think of returning. Her eyes moved from the now overcast sky, past the trees now completely in foliage, to the road where Max had stood that day. For one ghastly moment Kate thought she was having a genuine hallucination. Then, with a tremor, she realized, whatever her problems, they were not chimerical.

Max stood in the dirt road surveying her meadow.

Their eyes could not, at that distance, meet; yet Kate felt them meet. No worry this time about changing my clothes, she thought. Her pants were grubby as ever, and her shirt, a discarded one of Reed's, was tied up, leaving her middle bare. This she untied and tugged down around her hips in an act, she supposed, with some vestigial traces of the girding of one's loins. Max began to walk toward the cabin.

"Where to this time?" Kate asked as she opened the door to him. The thought of locking it occurred momentarily, only to be abandoned. He could always get in if he wanted to. And sooner or later she would have to talk to Max. How like him to have adopted the ritual of talking here.

"I'll sit at the table again," he said. "You sit where you like, of course. Do you think we might have some tea?"

"All right." Kate filled the kettle and put it on to boil. Waiting for it, she collapsed into her overstuffed chair and watched Max's inevitable lighting of his cigarette, the crossing of his legs. Like Noel Coward, she had thought, all that time ago.

He waited until the cups of tea were prepared, his in front of him, hers clutched in both hands as she sat, her feet beneath her, in the large chair.

"When had you planned your little exposure?" he asked.

"Any time would have done," Kate answered. "This as well as another, though it is hardly your style, Max."

"What made you take it up again, Kate, in your maddening female way?"

"How did you know I had taken it up? I've mentioned it to no one."

"No. I'm counting on the fact that you haven't. Not even to Reed, I'll dare say. Two fantastic tales are too many to spin inside one month, even to one's beloved and, if I may say so, ridiculously indulgent husband. I knew because Herbert told me, indirectly, of course. A very small piece of information will reveal a good deal to the person who knows how to use it.

"Herbert," Max went on, "was overcome with some impulse of fraternal feeling the other day. Perhaps you inspired it. We had dinner together at my club. He said how much he had enjoyed meeting you in Oxford, and how he had talked to you lately on the telephone. Oh, he didn't tell me your questions, Herbert is too discreet for that, but it was clear enough you had not relented in your feverish interest in my birth. This seemed to indicate you'd got hold of some further information you wanted to ratify. Am I wrong?"

"No. Quite right. Have you come, Max, because it gives you pleasure to dote on what a fool I've been, and how easily you manipulated me? I gave you every opportunity, of course. You couldn't have managed any of it without my eager help. I've tried to think where I first went astray. It was the portrait. That portrait made Whitmore so much more central, even in that house, than Cecily, who had died and removed the spirit. Do you think that's it?"

"No doubt."

"And after that I served all your purposes, from the identification of the body to the discovery of what I thought to be your mean and sinister motive."

"But it was all so complete, Kate. You had your letters, it was all so neat and finished off, with binding all around the edges. How did it happen to unravel?"

"Why should I tell you? My fatal desire to tell stories has done damage enough."

"Let's say because this will be the last one you ever tell."

Kate looked at Max. He had lit another cigarette, but barely sipped his tea. Was he noticeably less controlled? She must, at any rate, keep talking. She drew a cigarette from her pocket. "I won't light it yet," she said, as Max rose to his feet. "I'm still trying to give it up, as I told you last time." She held the pack of matches in her hand, playing with it.

"A while ago," she said, "just after you'd given me

the letters, a student came to see me. At home. I often see my dissertation students in the summer if I'm around; it's hard to deny them any consultation all during that time. Anyway, this young woman was one of those still searching around for a dissertation topic. She wasn't anyone I had uppermost in my mind then. One tends to focus one's attention on the students in one's classes or preparing before one's eyes for a crisis —an exam or essay." Kate wove her story on, aware of the necessity of talking, of going on talking.

"She had come to see me with her mind made up about a topic she wanted to propose. 'I want to write on Dorothy Whitmore,' she said. I expect I must have grimaced because she asked me if I had some objection to the topic. 'None that is important,' I said. 'No doubt I shy away from the subject because Gerry Marston was working on it.' She and Gerry had been together in a seminar of mine. 'Oh, no,' she said. 'Gerry was writing on Cecily Hutchins. She'd gone absolutely clunkers about her. Always had adored that sort of crisp novel, but when she came upon Hutchins, she just raced through everything from start to finish. It was Gerry, though, who put me on to Whitmore at first. Whitmore was much more my style. Not so much upper-class attitudes and wit and the right wine with everything.'

"I laughed, naturally, in that superior and maddening way professors have, and said I happened to know she was wrong. Gerry had definitely been working on Whitmore. Indeed, I could hardly be more certain of it.

"The young woman stared at me in some astonishment. One does not flatly contradict a senior professor who may be the sponsor of your dissertation, even if

200

she seems to have been going at it a bit hard and is manifesting the first signs of senility. Yet the young woman did continue to argue with me. The significance of that was slowly borne in upon me. If a student continues to argue with a professor, that student is pretty damn sure of her facts: I'd learned that early on.

"I told her, therefore, that I had perhaps been mistaken. We discussed Whitmore for a bit, and I told her what background material I thought she should look at. When she'd gone, I tried to think where I had got the idea so firmly in my mind that Gerry was working on Whitmore. I went back to my files, which I had not looked at since Gerry's death: all her letters to me, her proposal and outline and bibliography were there. No doubt whatever. Her dissertation had been Hutchins from beginning to end. The only mention of Whitmore came in a reference to Hutchins's friends and literary relationships.

"Don't think that at this point I felt any more than mild confusion. Obviously, there had to be some reason for my assumption that Gerry's passion had been for Whitmore. 'After all,' I thought to myself, 'I direct a great many students; this was a simple, not impossible, not even unlikely mistake.' But something had confirmed me in it. Not just the fascination of the portrait. Something else. Then, of course, Max, I remembered. It was that as yet unopened letter from Gerry at the Wallingford, proving Gerry was interested enough in Whitmore to have written Hutchins about her."

Kate paused. She lit her cigarette and made something of a business of looking for an ashtray. She discovered one and brought it back with her to her chair.

"Why don't you have a drink?" Max asked. "Are you still without anything but California wine?"

"I don't want a drink, thank you. Those unopened letters had rather troubled me the first time I saw them. It seemed such a loose end in an otherwise neatly handled estate. You must have kept them out to camouflage Gerry's letter—the letter supposed to have been from Gerry. You wanted my attention focused on Whitmore. Once that was clear, I compared the typing on that letter with Gerry's letters to me about her dissertation. The Wallingford letter had been typed on a different machine. That might not, in itself, have been court evidence, but it went a long way with me. You write other people's letters well, Max. How neatly you caught the bland tone of a well-mannered child writing to a famous author. And you succeeded in drawing my attention to the portrait, to Whitmore, and away from Cecily. Clean away from Cecily."

"You know what Wilde said." Max spoke now as though this were the sort of conversation dreamed about by aspirants to a world of style and high culture. " 'A man cannot be too careful in the choice of his enemies. I have not got one who is a fool. They are all men of some intellectual power, and consequently they all appreciate me.' A compliment to you, Kate."

"No, it's not," Kate said bluntly. "You thought you had one who was a fool. Clearly I did not appreciate you. But I admit the quotation as nicely chosen at this moment. You think all those who disagree with you are fools, Max."

"Do go on. Having compared the typeface according to the best rules of criminal investigation, what did you do next?"

"My governess used to do my hems. When I think of her now, that is how I always remember her. Being a woman of great neatness and conservative tendencies, in the best sense of the word, she would try to get out in one piece the thread with which the original hem had been sewn. She would try to catch it, and often it would break off. But sometimes the thread would come out perfectly and whole. She would wind it onto a piece of cardboard, feeling triumphant. This thread, Max, began to unravel in exactly the same way. Which reminds me, I've always meant to ask someone knowledgeable and devoted to the proper use of language: what is the difference between ravel and unravel, as in Shakespeare and the 'ravell'd sleave of care'?"

"Go on with your story."

It was an enormous effort not to show her fear. In refusing this digression, Max had told her much. There could be no question of his state of mind. For a moment she considered refusing to talk, but her only chance was if talk would distract him.

"What else is there to tell, Max? Nothing was left but the dissolution of my story. What an attractive story it was. And every piece of evidence, or what I chose to consider evidence, seemed to confirm it. Herbert was the one who showed me the folly of my ways. A few straight-forward questions and it became obvious that you were his real brother, not possibly adopted. He made clear, I blush to say, that adoption is a legal procedure and a matter of record. I asked if your mother might not have pretended to be pregnant: padding, travels, that sort of thing. It didn't take Herbert long to explode that theory. Then I realized that Whit-

203

more's medical record would have mentioned if she'd had a child. It's the sort of information doctors need.

"Oh, Max, how I admired the quickness of your responses. With what relief you must have heard that tale of your sinister parentage here, in this cabin, and realized that I had provided you with something you could not yourself have dreamed up; a safe motive. One, moreover, romantic and far-fetched enough to become mincemeat in the hands of any good defense lawyer. You could trust Reed and me to know that.

"I think of you, Max, those eight days at Raymond Brazen's—were you really at Brazen's, helping him with his book? That's one of the many points I haven't got around to checking."

"Oh, yes, I was there. I did help him with his book. But he is old and could only work a few hours a day. Moreover, bless the man, he is a keeper of inconsiderable trifles and always has been; one of those who can't throw anything away. He had paper that must have been many years old—old enough not to look the least new. The watermark worried me a bit; it might have been traced as an American paper. I put a bit in one of Whitmore's letters about her shortage of paper and her gratitude for the American paper Cecily had left on a visit."

"I think of you there, Max, writing those letters, copying that handwriting. You must have filched a few things from the Wallingford to copy from. Did you enjoy making those letters up? They were clever, Max. Damn clever. Except, as I realized later, Whitmore would never have wished for a boy that way or harped so on it. Women are not all as self-hating as you assume them to be; certainly not Whitmore."

"I was amused at how easy those letters were to write. I almost became Whitmore, dashing them off before rushing about, sticking her nose in where she wasn't wanted."

"Like Gerry Marston."

"Exactly like Gerry Marston."

"Why did you kill her, Max? Do you mind telling me?"

"Why should I mind?"

Kate had sometimes wondered how brave she would be if actually faced with violence. One never knew. Either one would be able to draw upon resources of stamina or one would collapse. Apparently she would not collapse. Her mind, moreover, seemed to have been sharpened by fear, at least temporarily. What she doubted now was how long she could resist the debilitating effects of fear.

"You realize that I shall kill you," Max said. "I must do that. But you will seem to have killed yourself." Kate noticed that even now he used "will" and "shall" correctly. We die, she thought, upon a fine point of grammar, and just avoided, almost too late, the tempting release of hysterical laughter.

"I don't in the least mind satisfying your curiosity," he continued. "Curiosity is an overpowering human motive, more forceful often than sex or money; it has not only killed the cat. Yes, light your own cigarette. I am much stronger than you might suppose, but you are tall for a woman and not overweight. There is something too vulnerable about a man lighting a woman's cigarette after he has threatened her life. Cecily and I quarreled. Before the wedding. She had asked me to come and see her not long before she left for England.

She had always said that I would be her literary executor, that I would write her biography. It was an established fact. Everyone knew. I had long arranged my life to include it. It had been agreed upon. After all, we had the same background, more or less, the same attitudes. So I thought. But Cecily turned out, when I went up there, to have transformed herself into one of those wide-eyed liberals, the sort who thinks students should be allowed to rampage on campuses and interfere with the workings of government and business. It emerged that we no longer saw eye to eye on anything. I said that at least she had been a good wife to Ricardo. 'Whatever do you think you mean by that, Max?' she asked. 'For many years I didn't live my life, I lived his. I bought his ties, and arranged his sittings, and massaged his ego, and organized his exhibitions. Oh, I wrote, but only when Ricardo was elsewhere, attended to by other and younger women who gladly ran his errands and did his chores and were content to worship him. Perhaps I was a good wife, but only after I became a good person, which was when we moved here permanently. Moved to the sea. After that, I didn't care if Ricardo came or not and, perversely, he used more and more to come. Those were our happiest years, when I ceased caring if I was a wife at all, and was often alone. Max, how much of everything do you understand? Do you think writing my biography is going to redeem that conventional, conservative, lost world for you?' 'You were a friend of my mother's,' I answered. 'I understand your life.' 'My God, Max,' she said, 'I don't think you understand anything. You don't even understand your mother.'

"We talked about everything then. Such conversations go from one thing to another, becoming worse and worse. Vietnam, Watergate, integration, women's rights —we covered it all. In the end she actually asked me to leave. Not then—it was late at night—but first thing in the morning. She said she was glad we'd had this talk before it was too late. 'How often,' she said, 'those who have affection for one another take for granted that they agree on important and fundamental things. You're wrong for me, as literary executor and certainly as biographer. I shall make that clear in my will. I'll write old thingybottom'—which is what she always called her lawyer—'the changes.' And that was all. The next morning I actually begged her to reconsider. She said there wasn't that much rush; plenty of time when she returned from the wedding.

"As you know, she died in England. Her children were abroad with her. There was the chance she'd said something to them, but it was unlikely. Cecily's charm had always been lost on her children. I think she had expended all there was in that way on Ricardo, whatever she chose to say later. I don't know how much Cecily delighted in her children, although they were very successful: Thad and Roger are with excellent firms, and the daughter made a very good marriage. Dear me, I'm wandering. There was a chance no one knew she had changed her mind. Up to the house I went, renting a car at the Boston airport, in another name, of course, and driving. Yes, I learned to drive, long ago, but why tell anyone? The Hertz people make it beautifully easy, as they say in their advertisements. I called ahead, reserving a car for Mr. Browning, and it was there. I gave them cash; they gave me the keys.

What could have been simpler? Before, I had stolen a driver's license from a stranger.

"Cecily had drafted a new section to her will dealing with her literary remains; she left it in the top drawer of her desk. It was the first thing you saw when you opened it. And I was not the only one who had opened it. Your Gerry Marston had opened it also. She swore she hadn't, swore she hadn't broken in, had found the back door opened, had only meant to peek and go to the bathroom, and somehow landed in Cecily's study. I found her looking at the portrait. A likely story."

"Not unlikely," Kate said. She herself had felt impelled to see Cecily's house, hadn't she? Hadn't that been one of her reasons for going with Max in the first place?

"Did you talk to her?" Kate asked.

"Oh, yes, we talked. I didn't accuse her of anything, or frighten her. I didn't try to make her admit she'd looked in drawers. I quite charmed her, if you want to know. Told her I was Cecily's literary executor and actually was interested in her theories and her work."

"What makes you think she read the draft of the will?"

"Her surprise when I told her I was literary executor. Her— It was obvious. Anyway, I couldn't afford to take a chance. And I couldn't afford to trust her. I ought not to have been there; supposedly I was around the university, between classes. I had a class next day."

"All that about the horse was nonsense, then?"

"Of course. My horsiness seemed to please you; it fit in nicely with Whitmore's horsiness."

"It wasn't hard, I suppose, to get her out on the rocks."

"Not particularly. Like you, she was longing to climb about on them. I joined her and pointed out something on the horizon. Then I hit her over the head with a rock. When she fell, I had to hold her head underwater. The tide was coming in, and did the rest. After that, I waited. The original will was prepared for probate. The lawyer informed me of what my duties would be. I knew then that it was all right. Except for the body."

Kate kept her eyes steadily on him. He needed no questions to continue.

"I didn't want a big brouhaha when the body was found. Nor did I want her to be missed, starting a big search from that end. In enticing you up there, my willing dear, to identify her, I took a chance. You might have been questioned anyway, once she was identified in that place, and this way I provided the groundwork for a perfectly natural explanation of her death. You didn't like it, I could see that, but your fascination with the Whitmore portrait helped me. Oh, Kate, you tried so hard to trust me, but you didn't. Not all my famous charm could change that. So when, finally, you came up with your wonderfully romantic story, quite worthy of the best in the Gothic novels, I was on to it like a shot. If Gerry Marston had been interested in Whitmore, as you so soon concluded, there was no way she could have possibly been a threat to me. You've seen that now. I quite enjoyed doing the letters, but I've told you that. I've told you everything, haven't I? I've talked too long."

"I have to go to the bathroom," Kate said.

"Do you? If this were one of the movies our crazed youth feed upon, I would watch you. But I don't care for that sort of thing. The window in there is too small and high for you to climb through. Close the door and be quick, do."

She did, indeed, need to go to the bathroom, but beyond that she had needed the respite from his presence. Yet this was a mistake. Out of sight of him, she became more nervous. Ought she try the window after all? "Coming out?" his voice called. She opened the door and moved back to her seat.

"Are you sure you wouldn't like a drink?" he asked. "No Scotch here anywhere?"

"None," Kate said. "Did you drive here?"

"Oh, yes, I've rented another car. But perhaps I shall soon admit to driving, when it's quite safe to do that, or perhaps I shall take very public driving lessons, at which I shall be inordinately stupid, and then I shall buy a car. I shall have more money now. You know, Kate, I'm not as well off as you suppose. When you drew all your lovely little conclusions about primogeniture, you were right. Herbert got the property, which was about all there was. I've already got an advance on this biography and a good contract. It will make money. Not, as you suppose, because it is about a woman, but because it is written well with true style and cynicism. I shall get reviews every bit as good as Malcolm Muggeridge's. We are the wave of the future, he and I; not, of course, that we have met."

She must keep him talking. That above all else was clear. "What are your plans?" she asked.

"To write the biography. To edit the rest, judiciously. And to expose the sealed Whitmore papers as spurious. I dare say any handwriting expert can help there. Let us only hope he is not clever enough to spot the real wielder of the pen."

"I meant your plans for me."

"I have a gun." Max brought it out and rested it on the table. "You can buy them, easily. You liberals who always want to license guns can't prevent that. If we all carried guns, and every crook and mugger knew it, there would be less crime."

"Am I supposed to have bought this gun?"

"Certainly. They wouldn't be able to trace it, but negative evidence is not conclusive. You've been gloomy lately. Taken to coming up here alone to brood. Worried about middle age, and the onrush of those who are younger. Disturbed, perhaps, by the death of a student."

"Am I to leave a note?"

"No. All that will be surmised. I have thought it through. No one will know I have been here. My car is hidden in the trees, away from the road. It will be one of thousands of cars returned to Hertz at the end of this weekend. The clerk will not even glance at me as she processes it. Oh, I thought of other forms of death. But the simplest is always the best."

"Unfortunately, there are no rocks."

"It would hardly have done to repeat oneself."

"And the old woman, Cecily's neighbor. She hadn't heard anything, or seen anything?"

"Of course not. But she is old and can be counted on to be forgetful, or to appear so. The lawyer had called me, as it happens, assuming I was still literary executor."

"Murderers always think they will get away with it. But something unexpected turns up. I promise you, Reed will never believe your suicide theory. He has

211

access to the most sophisticated of criminal investigations. Wouldn't it be safer to let me live?"

"No. I know your sort. I'd never be safe again, or think I was, which comes to the same thing. Oh, if you gave your word, perhaps, but you wouldn't. Would you promise?"

"To save my life? Of course. And keep it."

"No. You wouldn't mean it. It wouldn't count as a promise. You would persuade yourself that I had killed one person and might kill another. One can serve only one life sentence; one would have said 'die once,' before you liberals removed the death penalty."

With her eyes Kate measured the distance between them. If she began running wildly around, he could hardly shoot. One cannot be supposed to have shot oneself in the back. He had to be able to place the bullet where a suicide might have aimed it. That was on her side. She began to shift her weight in the chair.

"Don't move," he said. "My hope is to shoot you so that the wound looks self-inflicted, but if I must make it look like an intruder, I will. That is less to my purpose because it means that there is someone for whom the police are searching, but I will shoot you if you move."

"My feet are asleep."

"Stretch them in the chair."

"What time is it, Max?"

"Look at your own watch. What time does it say?"

"Five."

"What I have worked out," Max said, rising, the gun in his hand, "is that you would not shoot yourself here, in the cabin. You would not want to soil it for Reed, who after all, as you told me the first day I came here,

212

helped to build it and then bought it from Guy. You would walk deep into the woods. Then there would be one shot. Even if the local farmers noticed it, they would put it down to someone shooting a varmint. Allowable without a license, in any season. Let's walk out to the woods."

Kate, as she rose, willed her body to move, willed herself to rush him, to kick out at him, to tackle him. Too late now to think of all those courses in self-defense which had seemed aimed, somehow, at another generation, in a different sort of life. She could not will her body into combat, or even into a sudden motion. No doubt if he threw himself upon her, she would find the will for defense. But the initiative for a kung-fu leap through the air was beyond her.

He walked surely as they plunged into the woods; he had a compass. "There is always a danger, in woods, of walking in a circle, particularly when the woods are all evergreens," he said. "And I want to be able to get straight out. Immediately." They walked so far that it seemed to Kate they must be about to emerge at the other side, but her sense of time was betraying her in all probability. He kept motioning her on whenever she turned back to look at him. Ahead of him, she felt safer. He would not shoot her in the back if he could help it.

It was then that the surge of energy which is said to come to animals just before they die in a trap reached Kate. Within one enormous rush of vitality, she realized, her only chance was to run fast into the woods, to take a chance of losing him. Almost as her muscles tensed for the burst he called, "Don't run Kate, I will shoot." But she ran anyway, veering off sharply to one

213

side, hoping to get in back of him. And as she rushed, tripping over underbrush and banging into trees, she heard a shout and then the gun was fired. She was by no means certain if she had been shot, since she had run, the moment before, into a tree and been stunned.

"Kate," Reed's voice called. "Kate. Are you all right?"

"I'm fine," Kate said, and fainted.

"He's certainly mad," Reed said, sometime later, when she had achieved the house with the help of another man (what other man?) and Max, who had been knocked unconscious, had been carried off in an ambulance called by Reed at the telephone in the house of the woman down the road.

"I hope you paid her," Kate said, worried.

"I gave her ten dollars," Reed said. "Kate. Say hello to Guy. Between Guy and me, we overpowered him."

"Yes," Reed said, later still, when they were driving very slowly back to New York. "Of course I borrowed a police car, with flashing red light going like mad. We must have gone a hundred miles an hour. There's many a frightened driver along the Taconic Parkway who will not be the same for days. We did it in just under an hour."

"But how did you know?"

"Because, dear Kate, you are a woman of your word. Leo, with his blessed, wonderful athletics, called at three-thirty to say where were you? It was the last game of the season and you had promised to come, and he just wondered, weren't you coming? 'Did she say positively?' I asked, not really worried yet. 'Yes, I think so.

214

All the other parents are here. But it doesn't matter,' Leo said. 'I just wondered.' But he had run all the way to Fifth Avenue, when his team was up, to telephone.

"The game had started at three, which meant you must have planned to leave the country by one-thirty, two at the very latest. I told myself you had left late, your watch had stopped, you had run into traffic, there had been an accident, but it wasn't like you. You would have called or left a message for Leo. You don't leave people hanging, certainly not Leo. And you obviously had to come home first. So I went into your study and there it was, all the sorry evidence. I'd never been really happy about that story; not really happy. Max wasn't at home. That did it."

"And Guy?" Kate asked, so tired she could scarcely form the question.

"I needed help. I didn't want to shoot Max; that would have taken too much explaining. And Guy, in addition to being a revoltingly in-shape physical specimen, knew the cabin well and all its woody approaches. Not that we thought you would be in the woods; we decided to creep up on you that way. Then we heard him shout at you."

"And his gun just went off?"

"It just went off when we tackled him. The bullet went into the air and fell to earth I know not where."

"Imagine that," Kate said.

Later still, as they drove slowly down the Saw Mill River Parkway, Kate, who kept falling asleep against Reed, woke up and said, "So you never really believed in my romantic story. I thought it such a satisfactory explanation. To which, you will remember, Gwendolen returned: 'Yes dear, if you can believe him,' and

Cecily Cardew said: 'I don't. But that does not affect the wonderful beauty of his answer.' Didn't you think my story had a wonderful beauty?"

"What is she talking about?" Guy, who was driving, asked.

"No doubt it is a quotation," Reed said. "It almost always is."

"I do admire literary people," Guy said.

sixteen

Leo's graduation went off as well as could have been expected under the circumstances. Leo's experiences in his final term at St. Anthony's lent a certain hollow ring to the ceremony, which was followed, inevitably, by a hideous Fansler family luncheon. All the Fanslers were present, but Kate was at least able to become comfortably sozzled on champagne, an escape the graduation ceremony itself had not offered.

Leo had moved back to his father's house. As Reed and Kate finally bid goodbye to the assembled Fanslers, Leo thanked them for "everything," as though, Reed remarked, they had taken him for the afternoon to the zoo. They decided to walk down the Avenue.

"I haven't yet told you the final ironies," Reed said. "Finlay and Ricardo will doubtless both go to Harvard, one year late. There was never any doubt about Finlay; he is, as Leo kept telling us, a genius. And Max wrote such a moving letter on behalf of the Ricardo boy that Harvard has agreed to consider him most seriously. Max, no doubt, felt he had to keep on the good side of the family. The one who suffered in a sharp way was Leo: the headmaster stopped saying hello to him in the hall. I think Leo minded that."

"Crackthorne minded it, too," Kate said. Reed raised an interrogative eyebrow. "You know," Kate told him, "the young teacher who was writing a dissertation on the World War I generation; he who used to make the basketball games bearable. He's leaving St. Anthony's. I had a note from him. He said he's had enough expediency and sophistication to last him a lifetime."

"Kate, are you ever sorry you haven't been a parent for more than one year?"

"Nonsense. That's exactly the right amount of parenthood. Though, if I had to choose the year again, I would pick one with fewer events and crises. As Lady Bracknell observed in other connections, the crises this spring were considerably above the average that statistics have laid down for our guidance."

"You *are* all right, then. I always feel better when you quote Oscar Wilde. I've been a bit concerned about the possible aftereffects of being chased through a dark wood by a homicidal maniac."

"The habit of exaggeration is catching, I see. You know, Reed, I shall always wonder about Max. And when I am at the cabin, I shall always see him standing there, looking across the uncut meadow."

"We all live with ghosts," Reed said. "For me, at least, there will always be the ghost of Leo, not yet eighteen."

But the roster of ghosts was not complete. Some weeks later, after Kate and Reed had returned from a vacation abroad, an envelope was delivered from the Wallingford.

"To Kate from Tate," Sparrow had written. "Which is to say, not our official selves. This photograph turned up among Cecily's papers; I suspect Max meant to use it in the biography. I ought not, of course, to have had a copy made or to have sent it to anybody."

In the photograph, three girls posed for the camera, laughing, arms around each other's waists. On the back of the picture was written: "Tupe, Hutchins, Whitmore. Oxford, 1920."

The girls stood on a lawn, probably at Somerville, in the open sunlight. One could imagine, behind them, the dreaming spires.

About the Author

Amanda Cross is a pseudonym for a New York City university professor of English literature. She has written six Kate Fensler mysteries: IN THE LAST ANALYSIS, THE JAMES JOYCE MURDER, POETIC JUSTICE, THE THEBAN MYSTERIES, DEATH IN A TENURED POSITION, and THE QUESTION OF MAX.

MYSTERY
in the best 'whodunit' tradition...

AMANDA CROSS
The Kate Fansler Mysteries